A Far Journey

By

Ruth Ramsey

W & B Publishers
USA

W & B Publishers

For information:
W & B Publishers
9001 Ridge Hill Street
Kernersville, NC 27284

www.a-argusbooks.com

ISBN: 9781942981824

Book Cover designed by Dubya

Printed in the United States of America

Dedication

To my students, past and present, and to my family, the center of my life.

CHAPTER ONE

They said she went with tears to the altar— my mother. The good ladies of our town who had gathered to give us condolences said it in hushed whispers on the day of her funeral when they thought I wasn't listening. I heard them though. I had wandered into the big bedroom and had lain down, tired of the comings and goings of well-meaning neighbors and relatives and the constant grizzling of my brothers and sisters and the clucking of my aunts as they dealt with them. Daddy had gone off somewhere to deal with his sorrow, and I needed to be alone to deal with mine. Dazed with grief, I had wandered into my parents' bedroom and stretched out on their bed, covered with the patchwork quilt her hands had made, seeking peace, but I didn't find any. The running conversation in the front room made sure of that.

"Poor thing!" the disembodied voices whispered. The whispers hissed through the cracks in the door and seemed to echo from the tired pink roses of the floral wallpaper, becoming an accompaniment to the soft whisper of the rain outside. I listened without wanting to. The gossiping and condoling words floated round me and through me and into the black emptiness that threatened to swallow me alive. I buried my face in the patchwork quilt that still carried traces of her familiar scent, and wept.

***

I was fourteen the spring that my mother died, and the oldest of eight children born to her. They said that's what wore my mother out. Having all those children and taking care of them was too much for her heart. She had died in childbirth, giving birth to the ninth. The baby had died too. She and my mother were buried together, my mother's arms wrapped around her in eternal sleep.

***

Not knowing what else to do, I tried to step into her place. Taking care of all those children was almost too much for *my* heart. I felt as though I were one of those little burros I had read about in Geography class, burdened down with sacks and sacks of heavy rocks. The burden of caring for them was heavy. If my brothers and sisters weren't fighting, they needed a million little things. There was only me to provide them throughout the day because Daddy was usually off working, and when he wasn't working, he wasn't much help. He seemed lost without Mama to ground us all. He'd bury his face in his hands, and we kids would gather around him, mute with our own pain, but trying to comfort him in his.

"Ann Marie," he'd say when he finally did look up, "you've got to keep helping me out, now."

So I did the best I could, but I wasn't happy about it. It wasn't fair. Other girls my age only had to think about having fun and giggling about boys. My life now was changing diapers, cleaning house and trying to keep my brothers and sisters in line. While my friends swam and idled the summer away, I was saddled with the never-ending tasks of taking care of my brothers and sisters. My grief was an extra burden that threatened to swamp me at the least notice.

At night I crawled into bed exhausted, but unable to sleep, thinking of what had been said the day of the funeral by well-meaning ladies about my ability to cope with it all and wondering how much longer I actually could cope. My sisters and brothers were running me ragged.

There was Johnny, a skinny, freckled, redheaded, ten-year-old kid with a devil of a temper and a mouth to match. I guess he was just as angry in his way about losing Mama as I was. One thing was certain: He showed no hesitation about showing it. Half the time I wanted to hang him, and half the time I wanted to hug him. It depended on what mood he was in. Mostly, though, hanging won.

Georgie was eight and as quiet as his older brother was noisy. He was a smaller, softer version of Johnny, without the hair-trigger temper and sassy attitude. I didn't mind him so much. He minded me pretty well unless I or one of the other kids made him mad, and then he would take off somewhere, and I'd have to wonder where he was until he came back, because I couldn't go hunt him. He was prone to do that too, when the little ones all cried. I envied him that freedom and I wished I could do the same.

Janie and Lanie were six-year-old bundles of trouble. They had long, curly, blonde hair, angelic faces, big blue eyes, and, it seemed to me, one mind set on seeing how much mischief they could cause. People had a hard time telling them apart, and sometimes I did too. They took advantage of that—especially if one of them was in trouble. All one had to do was claim to be the other one. I finally told them that I didn't care which one did it, they were both going to get a walloping. Of course they tattled to Daddy, and then I would get in trouble. They drove me nearly crazy and they were the best advertisements for not having sisters I could think of.

Bobby and Joey were three and one and they took watching every minute. It was hard to get anything done because they got into everything. Sometimes I could get one of the bigger boys to entertain them, but it wasn't often. Johnny and Georgie had better things to do. Sometimes the little ones would be upset and would cry for Mama, and I would hold them and cry too, helpless to deal with their pain and mine, wishing that things were different.

Somehow or other, I managed to get us all through the days. The kids were fed and had clean clothes. The house wasn't perfect, but it wasn't dirty. Daddy started staying out later and later. Sometimes it was almost bedtime before he came home. About three months after Mama died, I got enough courage to ask him where he was all the time, and he told me not to be nosy. I had learned early in life not to cross him, so I swallowed my resentment and kept my wondering to myself. As time went on he seemed to be happier. He no longer sat with his head in his hands, and, once in a while, he even whistled. Then, one night in late August, he turned our world upside down again.

He usually was gone all day and part of the evening. It was usually nearly seven when I heard his old Ford pickup pulling in. To my surprise, he drove up early and he had a strange woman with him. I took one look, wondered who she was, and then had to go get Joey from under the bed, where he had gotten stuck and was bellowing at the top of his lungs. He did that about five times a day and never seemed to learn from the experience. Bobby was bouncing on the couch, and Janie and Lanie were having one of their screeching, hair-pulling fights. Johnny was God-knows-where, and Georgie – well, he had headed for the tree house just to get away from all the noise.

"Lanie! Janie! You stop that now!" I yelled, while fishing Joey from under the bed "You're going to fight with *me* in a minute and you know who's going to win! Be still, Joey!" I pulled my squirming baby brother from under the bed. He wailed because I had accidentally bumped his head in the process. Bobby chose that moment to fall off the couch and begin sobbing. Janie and Lanie were howling in rage. *A nice time to bring company home*, I thought.

"What's going on?" Daddy asked sternly as he opened the screen and held it for the woman, who came in and looked around at all the hubbub in astonishment.

Instantly Bobby went hurtling towards Daddy and wrapped his arms around Daddy's legs, babbling about what had just happened. Daddy lifted him up and hugged him. He buried his head in Daddy's shoulder and snuffled. Lanie and Janie forgot what they were fighting about and flew at him with happy shrieks. Daddy shifted Bobby in his arms and bent down to give them hugs and kisses. I just stood there, holding the baby. Once I had joined them in running to greet him, but now I was past the age when Daddy's coming home made everything all right the minute he appeared. Things hadn't been right since Mama died. I had given up expecting that they would.

The woman he had brought with him stood in Daddy's shadow, looking really little next to his lanky height. I wondered who she was. We didn't get very many visitors, and daddy wasn't in the habit of bringing strange females home. I wasn't sure I liked the thought of it.

"Thomas, he's adorable! And what a pair of little beauties!" she exclaimed, kneeling down on one knee, smiling at the twins. They beamed back at her, showing their dimples. They just *loved* being admired. *Pretty is as pretty does*, I thought sourly. This strange lady was about to be taken in.

The strange lady straightened and looked at me. *She* certainly wasn't very pretty. Her hair was dark brown and frizzy, as though she'd had a bad permanent. She had large, gray eyes set in a thin, pale face that ended in a pointy chin, sort of like a cat's face. She wasn't much bigger than I was, and I was small for my age. Her voice didn't fit her looks, though. Someone that looked like her should have had a high, whiny voice. Hers wasn't. It was almost musical, with a soft furry sound to it. That kind of voice should have belonged to someone who looked like a movie star, not to a skinny, little stick of a woman that a good puff of wind might blow away.

She was doing a great job of buttering the little ones up. Bobby was clinging to her skirts and looking at her with adoration. I hoped she wasn't going to try to butter me up as well. Her eyes, I saw now, weren't an ordinary gray. They were a funny, pale gray with dark rings around the outside of the irises, and they met my own resentful gaze coolly. I dropped my eyes as she turned her attention to Joey, who ducked his head into my shoulder and then peered at her, baby shy.

"This is Ann Marie, my oldest," Daddy said to fill the silence that had fallen. That's Joey she's holding. The little one there is Bobby," he had set Bobby down and Bobby was now tugging at her skirt. "Kids, this is Grace. Now, Bobby, leave Grace alone." He ruffled Bobby's hair and turned to me. "Ann Marie, where are Johnny and Georgie?"

"Georgie's in the tree house. He got sick of all

the noise. You know how he is. I think Johnny's out in the barn, killing frogs or bugs or something. Daddy, you need to have a talk with him. He won't mind me at all. Tells me I'm not his boss." I pushed a strand of hair out of my eyes, conscious of my rumpled cotton dress and uncombed mop of unruly, auburn curls that refused to look neat, even when I combed them, and that managed to work loose from the tightest ponytail. My usual end-of-the day messiness seemed worse when contrasted with the carefully groomed woman before me.

"We'll settle your problems later," Daddy said. Grace, who had turned her attention from Bobby to me, was now regarding me soberly. Daddy turned to the twins, who were simpering up at her. "Janie, you and Lanie run and fetch those two. I want them to meet Grace. She's been longing to meet all of you."

I couldn't imagine anyone longing to meet our bunch, and said so. Daddy sent a pained grin Grace's way and rolled his eyes.

She didn't say anything. She just stood there with a little half smile that made me squirm inside. I had a sudden desire to make that smile go away. I hoped the rest of the kids found the boys quickly so she could meet them. Maybe she'd leave then. After a day of wrestling with the bunch in question, I was in no mood to be polite and entertain company. I couldn't be rude though, or Daddy would have my hide.

"Have a seat, Grace." Daddy indicated the rocking chair in the corner. "It may take the girls a while to find Johnny. He's our wild man. He'll take some taming. Sure you're up to it?"

She sat down carefully and looked around again with that same assessing look that she had given me earlier, although she didn't answer him right away. The living room didn't look like much with its worn furniture and faded wallpaper. I was sure she was looking at it all and finding it wanting.

I looked from Daddy to Grace, not quite sure what to make of what Daddy had just said. What did he mean by her being up to taming Johnny? Was he going to send Johnny to live with her? Surely he wasn't. My heart felt as though a new hole had opened up in it. Johnny was a pest, but I didn't want him to go away.

"Well, I'll have to meet him first," she answered. Her words did nothing to soothe me. "I think that I'd better before I make any promises."

"Oh he's a terror!" Fear for Johnny's leaving made me blurt, "You wouldn't like him at all. He's got a mouth on him as big as Texas, and he's always picking fights with the others, or he runs off."

"Annie, why don't you let Grace make up her own mind," Daddy said, giving me a look that let me know I was stepping over the line. He turned to Grace. "She's had a hard time this summer," he said. "You'll have to excuse her. Would you like some tea while we wait? Annie, go get her a glass of tea."

"That's all right, I don't need anything right now," Grace said as she settled back in the rocker and extended her arms to Bobby, who was hovering at her knee. She certainly had made a hit with him. He crawled up into her lap and regarded her solemnly. She made a funny face at him, and he grinned.

I watched the exchange with resentment. *Daddy didn't have any call to point out what a hard time I was having,* I thought. I didn't want my troubles paraded before this strange woman. I remembered the gossips at Mama's funeral. What if she were like them and went around telling everyone about it? I hated being talked about. I sat down on the couch with a plop and set Joey on the floor. He immediately took off across the floor, toddling determinedly towards the two in the rocker. When he got there, Grace reached down and scooped him up to sit with Bobby on her lap. He grinned delightedly at her. I dropped my head so I didn't have to look at her and inspected my hands, as all sorts of dire scenes ran through my mind of our family's being split up.

It seemed like we waited forever for the boys to come, although, I suppose, it wasn't long. Daddy and Grace filled the time with chitchat. I listened half-heartedly, preoccupied with my thoughts. I was so deep into them that I nearly jumped out of my skin when the door opened with a loud bang, and Johnny came bursting in at full speed. He was covered from head to toe with mud and had a large, wiggling frog dangling by one leg from his hand. He skidded to a stop before Papa and was about to start running his mouth a mile a minute about his day when he spied Grace, who had recoiled at the sight of the frog that was struggling wildly to get free of his grasp. In his surprise, he stopped in the middle of a word and dropped the frog, which hopped away, to the wild dismay of the twins, who had come in the door behind him. Forgetting the frog for the moment, he stared at Grace, mouth open, while she struggled to compose herself. *Well*, I thought, *that was one way to make him shut up. Bring a strange person into the house.* Georgie opened the door at that moment and spied her as well. He stopped and then sidled in shyly, eyeing her as though she were some sort of sideshow freak.

"Who's that?" Johnny turned and demanded of me. I had to hand it to Johnny. Nothing kept him quiet very long. I shrugged and picked up Joey. All I knew was her first name and I didn't feel disposed to let him in on that. Let him find out for himself.

"This is Grace Smith," Papa said. "She wanted to meet you."

"Me? What for?" He eyed her suspiciously. "Are you some kind of truant officer or something?"

Trust Johnny to get straight to the heart of the matter.

Grace burst out laughing. She had a big, full laugh that sounded funny coming out of that thin, bony frame. "And what if I were?" she asked.

"John Bertrand Gibson! You been playing hooky?" Daddy roared, forgetting we had company and his need to keep up appearances in front of this woman, and completely forestalling any answer Johnny might have made. Johnny was immediately all wide-eyed innocence. He had never caught on that this sort of performance made him all the more of a suspect.

"No, Daddy. I was just asking." He returned to the attack. "What are you then?"

"Well, I'm not a truant officer. I'm just a normal, everyday lady. Thomas, why don't you tell him who I am?" She turned to Daddy, chuckling.

Johnny cocked his head to one side like a curious parakeet we'd had once and prepared to listen. I shifted the baby in my arms. *Yeah, who are you?* I thought.

"All right. I guess we'd better break it to them. I don't know any other way to do it. Come here, kids." Daddy put his arm around Grace. "I think happier days are going to be coming around this place. Grace has consented to be my wife." We all stared.

I couldn't believe my ears. Shocked, I stood up and carefully put the baby down. I was trembling so badly; I was afraid I'd drop him.

"No" I said. "No, no, no..." the words ran into a stream, and I was out the door, slamming the screen behind me, running as hard as I could, leaving Daddy's response to blow away in the sudden storm of my leaving.

CHAPTER TWO

I had a favorite place down by the creek that meandered lazily through the cotton fields near the place we lived. It was a perfect place to hide and daydream. It was a quiet spot, surrounded by elderly cottonwoods rooted deep into the blood-red clay of the creek side. I had found the spot when I was eight and claimed it for my own. I used to dream of being great jungle explorer and finding a lost city. I never found a lost city, but the lush growth of tall reeds and cattails made a perfect setting for a small girl's explorations. There I felt safe in letting my imagination run wild. As I had grown older, I often retreated there to think and to dream and to just get away from things. In my distress, my feet took me willy-nilly to my long-time refuge. I headed for it now, as a homing pigeon heads for home.

Over the years I had worn a path smooth between the trees and managed to clear out a little circle among the reeds that was perfect for hiding away when the mood suited me. Although I often went alone, I would sometimes let Johnny come along, if the mood suited me, and we would play at being pirates or enjoy a satisfying game of hide and seek. That was before he became a brat, and I got too big to play at such things. I hadn't had time to visit my secret place since Mama died. It hovered, however, on the edge of my mind, an oasis that offered solace.

I crashed through the last few yards of brush and reeds, heedless of the stinging scratches I was getting from the bushes that grew along the creek bank as they whipped my arms and legs and face. *How could anything hurt like what Daddy had said hurt? How could he even think of doing such a thing?* It was as though Mama were a puppy like we had had once. The puppy had died, and we had gotten another one to replace it. Mama hadn't even been gone five months yet, and there he was, bringing home another wife. It wasn't *right.*

Panting, I dropped to my knees and doubled over in a big knot of misery. If the earth had opened up and swallowed me right then, I wouldn't have cared. I don't know how long I stayed there, wrapped up in grief and anger, punching the ground in my rage, and crying rivers of tears, but gradually I became aware of a mockingbird singing in the branches overhead and the rustling sigh of the wind in the grass. I flopped forward onto my stomach and lay there listening, too worn out to do much else. I watched disinterestedly as a dragonfly skimmed over the surface of the muddy, red water that threw back sparkles of rippling light in the late evening sunshine. The peace of the place spread its calm over me. After a while, I fell into a dreamless sleep.

Johnny and Daddy woke me up, calling my name. I sat up in alarm. The sun had set during my sleep and around me everything was dark. I figured I was in some serious trouble. There was no telling how long Daddy had been looking for me, and I hadn't exactly been polite like Emily Post, the etiquette lady, before I took my leave. I toyed with the idea of not answering, but I decided that I'd only make things worse if I didn't. Besides, I didn't like the thought of being out all night alone. My refuge was creepy at night. I scratched at several new mosquito bites and called out, "I'm over here!"

"Ann Marie Gibson, don't you ever do anything like that again!" Daddy said as he came crashing through the bushes, set the lantern down that he was carrying, and pulled me to him. "I've never been so scared in all my life!" He held me back at arm's length, and gave me a slight shake. "We've been looking for hours. It's nearly midnight!"

I guess Daddy had forgotten I liked to come here. I was surprised he hadn't remembered.

"I'm sorry, Daddy. I fell asleep. I just needed to be alone for a while."

Daddy looked at me hard. In the flickering light of the lantern, he looked sad and stern all at once. I could tell he was weighing what to say. He rocked back on his heels and drew a deep breath. *Here it comes*, I thought. At least he didn't just up and whip me, but I figured I was in for one whale of a chewing out for scaring him so badly. Daddy had a pretty bad temper when pushed to the limit. He regarded me a for a moment, apparently trying to decide whether to be angry or relieved. Apparently relief won out. He sat down on the ground beside me. His tone was placating.

"Annie, I know you and your brothers and sisters have had a shock, me breaking the news like that. But you hadn't ought to be rude to Grace. She's a good lady and willing to marry a man with eight kids to take care of. Not many people would want to do that."

"Then what's wrong with her? There just has to be something wrong with her if she wants to take on a bunch of kids she doesn't know. Anyway, how can you just up and get married again? Mama's not been gone any time at all and here you are, bringing home a strange woman and wanting us to call *her 'Mama.'* Daddy, I *can't*!" The words poured out in a torrent. "Haven't I done good this summer? What do we need *her* for? I can take care of the kids. Tell her to go away! I..."

"Annie, *enough*." Daddy's voice, sharp as a steel knife, cut through the ribbon of my words and stopped me cold. "That's the whole point. *You can't.* I don't know what I was thinking of, leaving you to take care of everything. You're a child yourself. I've watched you getting thinner and worn out and crankier all summer, trying to do a grown woman's work. You're still just a kid. You've got school, and you ought to have a chance to do something besides take care of little ones."

His words echoed so exactly what I had thought so many times that summer that I was startled into silence. They were *my* thoughts though, and I didn't want them used as a reason to foist a new Mama on me. The thought of someone sitting in Mama's place at the table and using her things made me want to throw up. I hung my head, searching for the words that would get my feelings across to him.

"Maybe so, but I don't want to be the reason you replace Mama," I finally said. "Please don't make me the reason. Where'd you meet her anyway? A bar?"

Johnny's eyes flew wide open in shock at that. "Gosh, Annie! You don't mean that!" He shook his head.

I figured I did. I glared at him and Daddy, daring Daddy to deny it. *Where else could he have met her? What else could he have been doing, coming in all those late nights while I struggled with the kids?*

Daddy sighed. It seemed to come from the very tips of his toes and force its way out. I could tell by the way that his hands were clenching and unclenching that he was trying to keep control of his temper. He answered in the sort of calculated, patient tone that parents use to reason with unreasonable children when the parents are about to lose all patience with them. Since he was fixing to lose patience with me, I was pretty sure I was in for it.

"No, Annie, I didn't meet her at a *bar*. I didn't drink before your Mama died, and I sure don't now. I don't know why you would even think I would start. I met her when I was doing some work for her father over near Cloud Chief. I don't consider her a replacement for your Mama, as you so put it. No one could replace your Mama in my heart. I will always love her."

"Then how can you think of getting married again? You can't love her, then."

"I do love her, Annie. That's just it. I didn't plan on loving her. I just do. And she loves me. And she's willing to have me even though it means that she'll have to raise another woman's children."

"That makes it all right, I guess!"

"Annie, shut up!" Johnny never could stay out of a fight and I turned and glared at him. He regarded me solemnly. "I don't really like the idea any better than you do, but Daddy's right. You going to quit school to take care of us? You'd hate us all your days. You've not done nothing but yell and complain at us all summer because you had to take care of us."

His words stung with unadmitted truth. "Have not!"

"Have too! You're cranky and you're mean, and I'm tired of it." He scrunched up his face and balled his fists, ready to drive his side of the argument home and I stood ready to parry his onslaught. Daddy grabbed him before he could begin punching.

"YOU TWO STOP IT!" Daddy yelled. We knew better than to keep it up when he yelled like that, so we quieted down. We could argue later, when he wasn't listening. I glared at Johnny. I owed him two reckonings for that remark. I glared at him. *I'll deal with you later, brat!* He glared back, daring me to do something.

Daddy let go of Johnny, giving him a warning look and then took my chin in his hands and pinned my eyes with his. "That's enough," he said, when I would have pursued the point. "Let's get back to the house. And you, young lady, are going to apologize to Grace for being rude. No, I won't hear another word. I am marrying Grace. If you don't like it, I'll send you someplace else to live. I am marrying her and that's that." His patience was finally at an end. I knew it was useless to argue further or I would risk igniting his temper. I fell silent, but my anger burned. *Send me away?* How could he choose her over me? I guess I knew where I stood now. Sullenly I followed him, choking on the thousand unsaid things I wanted to say, back to the house.

The lights were burning in the kitchen and Grace was sitting alone at the kitchen table with a cup of coffee, resting her head in her hands. *Already made herself at home,* I thought. She jumped to her feet when she heard us come in the door. We stood there, awkwardly for a minute.

"I went ahead and fed the little ones and put them to bed for you," she said after a minute. "I've been keeping it warm in the oven." She indicated the stove. Johnny made a beeline for it, helped himself, and settled at the table to eat, wolfing down his food hungrily. I was too upset to think of food, and the last thing I wanted to do was eat what she had cooked. Daddy didn't seem too hungry at this point either.

"Thank you. I appreciate it. Annie here has something to say to you," Daddy said and pushed me forward. She looked at me inquiringly. I ducked my head and mumbled an apology.

"Louder!" he demanded.

"I'm sorry I ran off and left you with the kids," I said in a monotone. *There! She had her apology.* Daddy glared at me. This wasn't the apology he wanted. She frowned a bit at my tone and at the apology that really wasn't one, and I felt a little thrill of victory. At least I had gotten that silly smile off her face. It was a few minutes before she answered me. I ducked my head and stared at my toes, which were dirty from the creek bank. She reached out and lifted my chin so that she was looking fully into my face. I flinched away at her touch. *How dare she touch me?*

Disconcerted, she dropped her hand and stepped back. She stared at me thoughtfully for a few moments.

"I could say it's all right. But it really isn't, and you're not really sorry, so I don't want an apology. I can't blame you for how you feel, though. We'll talk later, but only if you really want to." Her eyes sought Daddy's and she shook her head ever so slightly, warning him against pushing the matter. When he would have said something, she stepped to him and placed a hand on his arm and whispered in his ear.

Having been ready to do battle, I didn't know what to think of her reaction. The last thing I had expected was understanding. I stood mutely, continuing to inspect my toes rather than keep looking at her. The last thing I wanted was to talk to *her*, ever. How I wished I could tell her so.

Daddy finally shrugged.

"Annie, you and Johnny run on up to bed. I'll deal with you later. I need to take Grace home now, Oh, and wash that mud off your feet, and face," he said. Careful to keep the mutiny out of my face, which was flaming with embarrassment, I followed Johnny upstairs. My scowling face warned him to keep his distance as we washed and got ready for bed.

Sensing my mood, he actually left me some hot water. I lay in the tub, wishing the water could wash the evening's events away like it did the mud. Downstairs I could hear Daddy and her talking. I wondered what they were talking about.

Later, as I lay in bed, I heard the pickup start up and drive away. I crawled out of bed and watched the truck go down the drive to the road. It seemed to me Daddy was driving away in more ways than one. It was as though he were driving away from me, too. I went back to bed and lay there for a long time, sleepless, tangled up in a mixture of grief and resentment.

"How could he? I'll never let her take your place, Mama. Never!" I murmured as I rolled over and punched the pillow. An eternity of sleeplessness later, I heard the sound of Daddy's driving up and the slap of the back screen door as it shut behind him. Outside, the locusts and crickets were singing the last of late summer song. I closed my eyes and allowed them to lull me to sleep.

CHAPTER THREE

I woke up with that disoriented feeling that a person gets when she's slept heavily, and a sudden feeling of dread overtook me. For a minute I cast about wondering why. Then I remembered. Today Daddy and Grace were getting married. For three weeks I had dreaded this day. I put my head back under the sheet and groaned. Maybe I could play sick so I didn't have to go with them to the preacher's house. At least they were making it a quiet wedding. *No need of making a big splash with Daddy's being so recently bereaved and all,* I thought bitterly as I sat up. It was only what others would say, I told myself. I'd have had more than that to say, but I wasn't asked, and I knew better than to say it—at least not out loud. It wouldn't have done any good anyway.

I crawled slowly out of bed and went to my dresser and looked into the mirror. I assessed the freckled, green-eyed image that stared back at me: scary, but too healthy-looking. They'd never believe I was sick. I picked up the brush and jerked it through the tangled morning mess of hair that radiated out wildly from my face. How, I hated that hair! My friends had nice smooth hair and skin that wasn't freckled. I looked like a sparrow's egg that had dark red yarn glued on it—nothing like Mama's creamy skin and dark blonde hair. Why couldn't I have looked like her? Instead, Daddy's red hair and freckles had been born again in me. I made a face and put the brush down. I would deal with the mess of my hair later. I bundled it into a messy ponytail at the base of my neck and bared my teeth at my reflection.

I could hear the little ones laughing and playing downstairs and the clink of dishes being set on the table and Daddy whistling. Apparently Daddy had gotten up before me and fixed breakfast. I wouldn't have to do that for once. I guessed he thought the extra sleep would improve my mood or something. I slipped into a pair of old blue shorts and a white crumpled blouse and clumped down the steps, giving the last one an extra hard thump. That was something I'd done ever since I was little. Mama and Daddy used to laugh at my doing that. They said it let them know I was coming. I still did it now, out of habit.

"Hi, Pumpkin. Have some breakfast." Daddy said, turning from the stove. He had made pancakes. He knew that was my favorite breakfast. I was startled at the endearment. It had been a long time since he called me that.

Okay, I thought, *butter me up. It won't work, but I'll eat the pancakes anyway since I'm hungry...on second thought...*

"I'm not hungry, Daddy." I slid into the chair and hung my head, glancing at him through my lashes to see how he took it.

"All right. Suit yourself." He turned back to the stove and flipped a pancake expertly. "But it's a long time until dinner." He didn't seem upset at all.

This definitely wasn't how I'd thought he'd react. He was supposed to be upset. I glared at his back. He was supposed to feel bad that I didn't eat. What good did it do to give up perfectly good pancakes to make a moral statement when the object of the statement didn't react? I slumped in my chair, looking gloomily at my plate in which two perfectly browned pancakes resided.

"They're real good, Annie!" Janie enthused, "I'll eat yours." She stuffed an extra-large piece of her pancake in her mouth and nearly choked. Georgie pounded her on the back. I offered her a sip of milk, which red-faced and coughing, she took. Her face scrunched up to cry, but a fierce glance from me quelled her. She began to eat again, sniffling a little.

I reached over and cut her pancake into smaller pieces. I had enough on my mind without the little pest choking to death. I'd probably get blamed.

"No, you won't! I will!" Johnny broke in, having downed the last of his. "I'm still hungry." He reached for the pancakes on my plate and I gave him a hard slap on the hand. "Oww!"

"Uh-uh, Johnnie. They are *mine*!" Lanie shrilled. It was her turn to receive my disapproval. She sat back and pouted at my look.

It was definitely a conspiracy to aggravate

me. Fed up, I rounded on the two latest offenders.

"You're both pigs! I didn't say I didn't want them. I said I wasn't hungry." I pushed the plate out of their reach.

"Well that's the same thing, ain't it?" Johnny scrunched up his nose, crossed his eyes, and stuck out his tongue at me. I wanted to smack him. Apparently, he thought his sole purpose in life was to make me miserable, and he was pretty darn good at it. Since Daddy was there, I settled for a hissed, "Shut up!"

"Annie, now, you don't need to be calling names. Johnny, you quit too. I have enough made that you don't need to eat hers. I used to be a boy once myself. Liked to eat a lot too. Guess you take after me, huh?" Daddy grinned at Johnny, and Johnny grinned back, Johnny's face a mirror image of Daddy's, only smaller. I suppressed the urge to roll my eyes.

"Now, you two hurry up and finish. I let you sleep late, Annie, but you've got to get a move on if we're going to get to the preacher's on time. Don't you even think of dragging your feet, girl." Daddy added, seeing my mutinous look.

I started to answer him back, but Joey started crying to get down. Leaving my uneaten pancakes on the table, I got up and lifted him out of the old high chair that had served each of us kids and cuddled him against me, kissing the soft baby fat at the nape of his neck, only to wind up holding him out from me when he returned my kiss with a syrupy one of his own.

"Yuck, Joey! You're all sticky! Sticky, sticky,

sticky, baby." I crooned as I carried him to the sink to wash his face and hands. He grinned delightedly and pat-a-caked, stopping to give his hands a solemn inspection when they stuck together and splaying them like miniature star fish as I placed his hands under the water.

"He'll probably need a bath," Daddy said. "Give him to me. I'll get the boys ready as soon as I get this mess cleaned up. You get the girls ready." *This must be a really special occasion. He never washes the dishes,* I thought.

"I'd rather help the boys," I said. The little girls were real pains to get ready to go anywhere. They whined about having their hair brushed and complained and got into snits about everything. I hoped I never had a little girl when I got married, if Janie and Lanie were any indication of what was in store. I sighed, "All right you two, get upstairs and let's see if we can get you ready." I herded them up the stairs.

By the time I had brushed out their hair and had gotten them dressed in their new dresses, I was ready to kill them. After admiring themselves in the mirror, and arguing over who was prettier— a waste of time really since they were so alike— and prissing around a little bit, they climbed on the bed and started bouncing crazily, unmindful of their finery.

"You're going to tear your dresses! Stop bouncing on the bed! You are going break it! Do you want to sleep on the floor?"

"Nooo!" They shrieked, but kept bouncing,

gold ringlets flying. I decided to let them learn the hard way when the old bed caved in. I had. They weren't going to get any pity from me when they hit the floor either. I hoped they learned a hard lesson. I turned back to the mirror and began trying to tame my hair. Like the girls, it refused to cooperate.

"Going to a wedding! Going to a wedding! Going to a wedding!" They chanted with each bounce. Out of patience with them, and with my hair, which continued to stick out in odd places, I finally snapped.

"Will you QUIT?" I shouted. They immediately started to cry loudly enough to wake the dead.

"What's going on up there?" Daddy yelled from the foot of the stairs.

"Daddy, they are being brats, and I'm sending them down there. If you want me to get ready on time, they've got to get out of here." I called. I turned to the girls. "Get out of here, you little demons!" I hissed.

"Daddy! Annie called us a name!" Janie shrieked in a tone calculated to burst my eardrums. She ducked the ear-boxing I aimed in her direction and flounced out of the room, closely followed by Janie, who gave me a wide berth. I grinned at them evilly.

"She's been doing a *lot* of name calling this morning. Come on down and leave her alone a while before she does worse to you," Daddy called. "Get a move on, Annie!"

"All right! All Right!" I gave a few final

swipes to my hair with the brush and tied it back with a big blue ribbon. A few rebellious strands had already escaped. I hoped it would stay put at least until the ordeal of the ceremony was done. It was bad enough to go to a wedding one didn't want to go to without a person's hair's resembling a tumbleweed. I wished Daddy would let me cut that mop.

I gave a final twitch to my dress and took a minute to smooth the folds. I didn't like the thought of his marrying Grace, but the dress she had made me was a dream in blue eyelet and lace and was the prettiest thing I'd ever owned. The gathered skirt billowed out in a cloud from the cap-sleeved, sweetheart necked bodice. She must have worked for hours and hours to make both this one and the dresses that the little girls were in danger of ruining. Too bad all this finery was going to be wasted just on the preacher and his wife and Grace's parents.

I was glad Grandma Jenkins wasn't around. It would have been uncomfortable for sure to see your son-in-law marrying another woman.

Grandma Jenkins didn't live that far away, but she and Daddy didn't see eye to eye on a lot of things. She had had some sharp things to say when she came for a visit and found out that her son-in-law was remarrying—things that he felt had to listen to since she was his mother-in-law and he owed her that respect, but that he didn't like at all. He had listened in an icy, polite silence that let me know he was working hard to rein in his temper. Then he asked her to leave.

She left in a huff. Daddy, in his anger, and to my dismay, vowed that we wouldn't see her again, but Grace, who had been an unwilling witness to the scene, had stepped in and told him that what he was considering was wrong, that she would probably feel the same way if she were in Mrs. Jenkins' shoes. He finally calmed down and admitted he was wrong. The kids had lost their mother, and they needed their grandmother, however irritating she was.

Although I didn't like Grace, I felt a grudging admiration for her. She apparently knew how to reason with Daddy. My Grandma Jenkins didn't.

Remembering that scene, I turned from side to side, enjoying the satisfying swish of the dress. A pair of strapped, dainty, white sandals completed the outfit. I had wanted a hat, but Grace had said that wasn't suitable for a young girl and made me a hairpiece trimmed with blue flowers. They perched there precariously on the knot of gathered hair at the back of my head. In spite of who had made it, I wasn't going to turn down a new dress. Those didn't come often. Sometimes I had hand-me-downs from the cousins. They were nice dresses, but they weren't new. Mama hadn't had much patience for sewing, but then, she had too many kids to take care of to have time to do it, I thought, feeling guilty for comparing her to Grace and having Grace come up looking better. "Sorry, Mama," I whispered in case she might listening, and then hurried downstairs to repair the damage the girls had done to their hair and dresses with all their bouncing. I wasn't gentle. It was bad enough I'd had to get them ready once. Twice was too much. I gave each a swat on the behind and sent them out to the car. They flounced out.

Grace's father had come to get some of us while I was getting dressed. He was a big, hearty man with a pot belly and a bald head fringed by silver gray hair. Daddy joined him, dressed in a nice gray suit. I stared. I had never seen Daddy in a suit before, even on the occasions when Mama had managed to wrangle him in going to church. He said he had had enough of uniforms when he was in the service. He had only worn a nice dress shirt and pants to Mama's funeral. He greeted Mr. Smith, who laughed and slapped him on the back and then turned to me.

"Well, look at you! Who is this lovely young lady? Tom, you're going to have to get your shotgun out to keep the boys away!" he said.

I thought that he was laying it on a bit thick, but it was nice to be called pretty. I blushed, and he smiled. I noticed that Grace shared his eyes. They were keen and considering. Neither his nor hers missed much, I thought as we trailed in his wake out to the car, a shiny blue Ford Fairlane.

He loaded us girls into the back seat, and put Johnny and Georgie in the front with him. Johnny promptly turned around and grinned triumphantly at being able to ride shot-gun. He shot me a thumbs-up. George climbed in and sat quietly, staring straight ahead. I wondered what he was thinking. Mr. Smith climbed in and waved at

Daddy, who was loading Joey into the pickup. I was glad I didn't have to ride in it today. It was bad enough to go to a wedding you didn't want to go to, without looking ridiculous in the bargain. I smoothed the folds of my skirt to keep them from wrinkling and then busied myself with the girls, doing the same. They were going to arrive in some sort of order, if I had anything to do with it. I wasn't going to give anyone any reason to say I couldn't cope on my own with them.

We didn't go places very often now because our old station wagon had broken down last spring before Mama died, and then Daddy had gotten the pickup so he could go to work. Most of us could ride in the back, he said, and he could haul things. Mostly he just hauled things. We didn't go places very often, now because even with some of us riding in the back, there were still too many of us. I didn't see why Daddy at least didn't trade for a station wagon so he could haul all of us kids and we could actually go somewhere. Besides, I was getting too big to ride in back.

I could just hear the hoots of laughter from the kids at school in the fall if I rode up to high school in the back of a pick-up. I cringed at the thought of arriving in that way, as I settled myself into the back seat of the car, gave my skirts one last smoothing, and elbowed Janie, who was flouncing excitedly, to make her sit still.

She slid closer to Lanie, and folded her arms and pouted, shooting me looks that could kill, kicking the back of the seat with her feet. She quit when Mr. Smith turned and looked at her warningly. One of the white patent leather shoes Grace had gotten for her already had a big scuff mark on it. She busied herself trying to wipe it off. At least she wasn't making noise.

Grace and her mother were already there at the preacher's house when we arrived. Her parents, the only ones present besides the preacher and his wife, were going to witness the wedding. *As if seven kids aren't enough witnesses*, I thought. I wondered what the Smiths thought of getting so many new step-grandchildren at once. I couldn't tell from their behavior that they were upset. Mrs. Smith fussed over the little ones and gave each of us a hug and told us to call her "Nannie." Johnny actually allowed her to hug him without a rude comment. I made a mental note to take Johnny's temperature when we got home. That certainly wasn't normal behavior for him at all.

The Smiths were staying with us a few days while Daddy and Grace went on a wedding trip to Oklahoma City. I figured the Smiths would learn about Johnny soon enough. He had latched on to Mr. Smith, and was pestering him with his usual hundred and twenty questions. The funny thing was that Mr. Smith didn't seem to mind. He was laughing and pestering Johnny right back. Johnny's rowdiness didn't seem to bother him at all. Mr. Smith and Daddy seemed to get along well too.

I hung back and trailed behind everyone as we went into the house where the preacher and his wife were waiting with Grace. Grace smiled when she saw Daddy, her face lighting up. It made me uncomfortable. Mama used to look at Daddy like that. My heart felt as though it had been stabbed. *I'm not going to cry!* I told myself fiercely. I pretended something was in my eyes and rubbed them. This earned me a sharp glance from the preacher's wife, who was far too nosy for my liking. She always cornered me at church and asked uncomfortable questions that I didn't want to answer about how we were doing. I wondered what she thought about this hasty wedding. I decided I didn't want to know. I hid my hands in the folds of my skirt and clenched my fists until they hurt to match the pain I felt.

I was glad that the ceremony didn't last very long. I had to bite my tongue when the preacher asked if anyone had any objections. I had plenty. I opened my mouth, but caught the preacher's wife looking at me again, so I turned it into a yawn. We had been talked enough about, I thought. I didn't need to give Pastor Snow's wife any more reason to talk. She already had had enough to talk about—she and the rest of the congregation. I could just hear her telling every little detail of the wedding to her friends at the next church social. Not that she could find anything to fault in the way Grace was dressed. It was a creamy beige lace confection of a dress with a little pill-box hat to top it off. She may have been skinny and not real pretty, I thought grudgingly, but she did have style.

As the pastor conducted the service, I let my mind wander to the church we usually attended. I used to like going to church. I liked the bright light filtering in through the stained-glassed windowpanes and the soft organ music and the singing, but when the word got out about Daddy and Grace, sitting in church had become an ordeal. Daddy had no idea what an ordeal it was, since he dropped us older kids at the door and drove off, leaving us to endure people's looking at us kids and whispering about us when they thought we weren't looking.

I could just imagine what they were saying—things like "She's not even cold, yet," and "He was sure in a hurry, wasn't he?" Even worse were the ones who pretended that everything was normal, but you could tell they didn't think it was. I had pretended I didn't notice, but I did, and it hurt. It was really hard to concentrate on what the preacher was saying when you had all those curious eyes boring into your back. I lapsed into a daydream in which Mama, who had been feisty and didn't put up with much, was telling those people to mind their own business and leave her girl alone.

I was jerked out of this satisfying daydream by the final words of the marriage ceremony: "I now pronounce you, man and wife." Daddy was kissing Grace. The ceremony was over. Mama wasn't there. In her place was this woman, and she was Daddy's wife now. For better or worse I now had a stepmother.

CHAPTER FOUR

"Hey, Annie! Where're ya going?" A shrill, slightly nasal voice broke into my thoughts. I had been scuffing along the pavement, absently kicking a rock, deep in thought. I had just gotten off the bus and was putting off the scary task of going up to the doors for my first day of high school. I wasn't sure I was ready. I looked up. It was Sally Moore. If I hadn't recognized her voice, I wouldn't have known her. Over the summer she had grown three inches taller and sprouted curves. Her hair was artfully arranged in the latest style and she wore a sweater set to die for. She had transformed, and looked ready to take the school by storm.

"Wow, Sally! What'd you do to yourself?"

"Like how I look? Well, you'd have known if you ever came around," She twirled in front of me and minced back to look me in the eye. "Where have you been?"

I stared at her in disbelief. How could she ask that? Didn't she know? It wasn't as if she had talked to *me* all summer. In fact, no one had even come around.

"Taking care of brats all summer. What do you think?" I said, conscious of my wild, red mop and my unfashionable skirt and blouse that tended to become untucked from the waistband, and determined not to let her know how envious I was.

"Tough break!" She sympathized insincerely and began to hum as she fell in step beside me.

I winced. Her singing skills didn't match her looks. What she could do to a song defied description. Hoping to stop the singing, I asked, "What'd *you* do all summer?"

"Oh, I swam, and I met the most *divine* boy when me and my parents went on vacation!" She trilled.

"Where'd you go?"

"We went to Yellowstone," she signed gustily. "I met him there. He was so dreamy! He promised to write me and he did!"

I had a momentary vision of Sally and Smokey the Bear kissing. "Love among the geysers, huh?" I muttered, having read a little about Yellowstone. I was really eaten up with envy then, thinking she had gotten to go someplace like that, and I was somewhat disgusted that all she could tell me about the trip was that she met a boy. I would have killed just to get to go somewhere far-off and exotic like that instead of being stuck at home.

"Was he named Smokey?" I asked sourly.

"I declare, Annie, you've turned just plain hateful," she flounced on ahead to a couple of friends she had spied walking ahead of us, shooting me a look of pure indignation. They began chattering together, like a flock of twin-setted, pastel magpies.

I sighed. I had too much on my mind to worry about Sally Moore and her love life, or my love life, or lack of one if it came to that. I had Grace on my mind. She was in the process of rearranging the whole of my life.

She had walked carefully the first couple of weeks after she moved into the house with us. Then, little by little, she had begun to change things. Mama's whatnots and pictures were stored "in a safe place for you girls" and her stuff went up on the walls, which she had painted and re-papered. It didn't feel like home any more. It was like losing Mama all over again. At least she left my bedroom alone. I think she knew she would have had war if she had tried to redecorate there.

When I protested, Daddy told me to shut up. It was natural, he said, that she didn't want to live among things that belonged to another woman. I asked him why she didn't just store us kids in a safe place too.

He lost his temper at that and we had a really bad fight. I ended up in my room nursing a sore heart and vowing to run away, and he didn't speak to me for days. It wasn't the first fight we had had since Grace had come into our lives. In fact, it seemed like all Daddy and I did was fight any more. It was all *her* fault.

Then there was the way she took over the little ones. It nearly broke my heart for them to look at her and call her "Mama."

She's not your Mama! I cried silently inside myself. *Don't call her that.* They were so little they wouldn't remember our Mama. I vowed to myself to always speak of her to them. *They should know that Grace wasn't really their Mama,* I thought.

She fussed over the twins and dressed them like little dolls. They had started their first day of school in brand new dresses and saddle shoes. They loved the attention and adored her. They didn't seem to mind this new woman masquerading as their mother, I thought, giving another rock an extra hard kick and wrapping my arms close around myself. *Little traitors.*

Georgie didn't say much. He kept things close to himself—too close. He didn't take up with her, but he didn't express any anger about it either. He was even more silent than he used to be, but I would hear him crying into his pillow at night and go to him and hold him.

Johnny was, well, Johnny. He kept his grief to himself. He was practical about Grace's entrance into our lives, and didn't let that keep him from continuing to make my life miserable. At least he dealt out equal misery to her once the novelty of having a new stepmother wore off. She spent a good deal of time trying to teach him to be civilized. She didn't always succeed.

I wasn't sure anyone would. I kept him in line by pummeling him from time to time—just for the principle of the thing, not out of any true desire to make him mind her—which got me in trouble.

Me, I hovered just on the edge of rudeness. I wanted to provoke her if I could. The trouble was, I hadn't been able to succeed. She just looked at me when I got rude. I hated it when she looked at me like that. She gave no sign of hurt feelings, just looked at me like she was taking stock and hadn't found much. It drove me nearly wild. She spoke no more to me than necessary, but she was pleasant and polite. Every effort I had made to get her goat failed. She never had to tell Daddy how I acted either. The other kids took care of that and then he lowered the boom. I hated them all, I decided.

I was so preoccupied with my thoughts that I missed the first step in the flight of stairs leading to the main door of the high school and tripped. I wound up sprawling on the steps with my supplies flung everywhere. A group of boys and girls standing to one side laughed. I got up, face flaming, and gathered my scattered things. None of them moved to help me. The first day of high school and I was getting off to a really good start, I fumed. *I'll never live this down.*

"Hey, look at that! Her face matches her hair!" A tall boy with a letter jacket jibed.

"There's a step there!" Another boy called out.

"Her name must be Grace!"

No, that's my stepmother. Mortified, I brushed at my skirt, and picked up my stacked notebooks. It was bad enough to look like a scarecrow, and then to fall on my face was almost too much. I rushed up the stairs and into the door, only to bump into a girl coming out at the same time.

"Excuse me," She and I mumbled and moved to one side—the same side of course. In spite of myself, a smile began at the corners of my mouth. It felt strange, that smile. I suddenly realized that I hadn't smiled in a long time.

She smiled back and giggled a bit.

"Well, I guess bumping into someone is one way to meet a friend. I'm new here. I'm Patty. I'm new in town. Who are you?" She stuck out a plump, well-manicured hand and, warming to her, I took it, somewhat embarrassed at the state of my hands with their chewed fingernails and reddened skin.

"Ann Marie, but call me Annie. Uh, we better get out of the door. The bell's fixing to ring and we'll be flattened if we stand here."

We stepped inside the door and started down the hall, moving with the flood of students coming in the door. "

What grade are you in?"

"I'm a lowly freshman, and I'm scared to death!" she rolled big blue eyes fringed with golden lashes at me and gave a little bounce that made the curled blond bangs that fringed her forehead flop up and down. "I don't know anyone here, but look out! I'm going to!" she declared.

I decided she might be fun to know. I shoved my dark thoughts aside and smiled at her earnestness. "Me too. And I just did a three-point landing on the stairs. All the upper class guys were laughing at me."

"Oh how awful!" She gasped. "I'll bet that's why you were coming in the door like a pack of wolves was after you."

"Yeah," I admitted sheepishly. I bent down and lifted the edge of the skirt to assess the damage done to my knees, which ached ferociously. They were skinned, of course. I hoped they wouldn't drip blood down my legs. That's all I needed.

"Those look painful and I'm sorry you are hurt, but well, I'm glad you did fall down and rush in here. We wouldn't have run into each other if you hadn't." She looked at me sidewise and grinned.

I grinned back. Maybe high school wouldn't be so bad after all; especially if you could make a new friend who made you smile in spite of embarrassing spills and skinned knees.

The bell rang.

"What class do you have? I've got Oldham for English in Room 12. Do you know where that is?" Sally asked.

"It's downstairs. I have English that hour too. Looks like we have that together. Do you like English? I've heard Mrs. Oldham is a hard teacher and makes you write a lot." I had heard this from the older girls at church, who spent lots of time, when they weren't talking about boys, complaining about their teachers.

"I hate English and I hate writing in particular. I can't make sense of those nouns and verbs and things, either."

"Well, I hate math. I don't like numbers."

"I'm pretty good at math. Numbers are beautiful," she declared.

I rolled my eyes at that. "I'm pretty good at English. Words are beautiful,"

It was her turn to roll her eyes.

I laughed. She understood my sense of humor. None of my classmates did. It would be nice to have someone who laughed at my teasing.

"Hey! Sounds like we could help each other," she enthused. "I knew there was a reason you ran into me."

"Maybe we can. When it comes to math, I need all the help I can get," I replied. "I've never been any good at it."

"Come on, then. Let's hurry and get this first day over with. If I fall asleep, poke me." She was off and skipping down the stairs to our first hour class, which was in the basement of the building, two at a time under the disapproving eye of a hall-monitoring teacher, who immediately told her to stop it. I hurried to catch up. Maybe I'd get through the rest of the first day of high school whole, I thought. Patty would definitely make the first day interesting.

By three o'clock Patty and I had formed a good beginning to a close friendship. She had moved to town from Kansas because her father had bought the local drug store. She said she had never seen such a small town. I told her that this small town was all I knew, and she said we would have to fix that. She told me about her family. She was an only child. I looked at her half-enviously.

What would it be like not to share every waking moment with a bunch of babies? She, in turn, was curious about my family.

"Oh, there's a bunch of us," I said airily. "Seven of us kids, to be exact."

"Wow. That really is a bunch. Want to rent a couple to me? I'd like a brother or sister," she said wistfully. I stared at her incredulously.

"Patty, I wouldn't wish my brothers and sisters on just anyone...maybe my worst enemy once in a while, but certainly not on you. They're brats," I said.

"Well, I'd like to meet them. I love little kids."

"I'd like them better if there weren't so many of them. They can be awful at times." I thought of my brothers and sisters ruefully. It was a new idea to me that little kids could be loved just for being little kids. To me, they were a daily nuisance.

"Do you want to go downtown and get a Coke after school. My dad will give us one on the house."

"Gosh, I'd better not. I've got to help my stepmother do laundry or my daddy will be mad."

"You have a stepmother? Is she wicked?" She asked archly. "You sound like Cinderella."

Wow, she is close to the truth, I thought. I did have to do most of the chores while Lanie and Janie prissed around and were adored. Of course, they were real sisters instead of steps. I considered answering, "Yes." But Grace wasn't really wicked. She just wasn't someone I wanted. "No, not really. But she's kind of different. I don't know what to make of her at times."

"Oh," Patty consulted her watch. "Well, I guess we better get to class. We don't have any classes together this afternoon until music. Drat the luck. You want to meet me at the front steps?"

"Sure," I watched her as she walked away. I appreciated the fact that she didn't pry. She just might make a decent friend after all. It didn't seem to matter to her that I was no fashion plate.

In fact, when Sally and her group had spied her and come twittering around and asking Patty questions, she had just looked them up and down. She had been friendly, but not as friendly as she had been with me. I could see they irritated her with their talk of dresses and boyfriends and their flouncing around. She was dressed just as nicely as they were, but she wore her clothes as clothes, not a costume.

I wished I could have some of her flair in dressing. Maybe she could help me with that. With a final wave, I headed to class.

Later, on the bus ride home, I thought about the day's events. I really liked her. I wished I could have gone and had a Coke. *Drat the laundry*! If Daddy hadn't threatened me with doom and destruction, I'd have let Grace do it all herself.

When I got home, I found Grace bent over the rinse tub of the wringer-washer and running clothes through the wringer before she hung them out. She was hot and sweating and her hair was curling damply in dark tendrils around her flushed face.

Joey was sitting nearby playing with a pan and a spoon. He looked up and flashed me a dimpled smile that was Mama all over again. I caught my breath at the pain of it, then stooped down and kissed him. He reached up chubby arms and I picked him up, cradling him close. Later he would be a pain, but right now he was all sweetness. I gave him smacking kisses all over his face, making him giggle, and then set him down and gave him his pan and spoon again.

I stared at the remaining piles of laundry with distaste. Ten people produced an awful lot of laundry. I knew there would be sessions at the ironing board to follow. I hated ironing even worse than laundry.

"You run on upstairs and change clothes. I'm about ready to have a load of laundry to hang out. I've been at it all day and I'm bushed." Grace wiped a hand over her forehead and straightened up. "We can maybe get this load out on the line so you can have clean sheets tonight, if you hurry."

That was Grace's way. She never let on that I was dawdling, just put it in terms that forced one to have to hurry up. I went on up the stairs and changed into an old pair of jeans and a shirt. It was much cooler that way. I hung up the skirt and shirt I'd been wearing, wishing for one of those pretty twin sets everyone else was wearing, and then made my usual way down the stairs, landing with the accustomed thump.

She looked up sharply and then arranged her face in a neutral expression.

You didn't like that, did you? Good! I thought. I started taking the clothes out of the rinse water and running them through the wringer, trying not to catch my fingers in the rollers. I'd done that once, and, ever since, I'd been on my guard with the pesky machine. For a while we were busy with wringing out the last of the clothes and draining the water and emptying the tubs. Then when I was heading out the door, with the damp clothes in a basket, she suddenly said, "How old are you, Annie?"

"I thought you knew? I'm fourteen." *She had to ask?*

"You're getting to be a young lady now," She paused before going on, long enough for me to get her meaning. I wasn't supposed to be thumping downstairs. "Your daddy didn't tell me when your birthday was."

"It's Christmas Day. I was his and Mama's Christmas present," I said deliberately, seeing if she would react to the dig. In true Grace fashion, she didn't. I thought I'd have liked her better if she had lost her temper just once, or didn't hint to me about thumping down the stairs, but just said she didn't like it out loud.

"Well, I'm sure that was the nicest Christmas present they could have had." Bent over the wash, she didn't see me making a face. "I've been thinking. How would you like one of those new matching twin things that the girls are all wearing now?

How would I like one? I'd have died for one, but I wasn't about to tell her that.

"I wouldn't mind," I said noncommittally.

"Annie, you've been such a help, I'd like to take you into town and treat you to a new dress and a visit to the beauty shop. Ever been?"

I turned around and set the basket down, eyeing her suspiciously. "No. I never have. Why?"

"Oh, no reason. I just thought a young lady might like to visit the beauty shop. I'm going and I wondered if you might want to go along too, and if you see a hairdo you want...well, call it a present for working so hard to help me around here."

"You don't have to buy my help," I said stiffly, picking up the basket. I heard her sigh.

"Annie, look at me."

I did, meeting her eyes squarely. The sadness in them caught me off guard.

"Annie, why do you have to make the simplest things into a battle? Can't you let me be a little good to you? It doesn't mean I want to buy you. I just want to see you a little happier."

"There's nothing you can do to make me happier." Why can't you just leave me alone?" I flounced out the door. "I'm fine the way I am."

Outside in the yard, I felt kind of ashamed. There she was offering me the two desires of my heart and I couldn't even swallow my pride and anger enough to accept them. I couldn't just go back in now and say I was sorry. Then she'd think it was for the new dress and the hair do. I plopped the basket down and began hanging up clothes, jabbing the clothespins on the line savagely. Why couldn't she just leave well enough alone?

I should have let her take me to town and get my hair cut. That would have irritated Daddy no end since he didn't like short hair. I lost myself in a haze of satisfying scenes in which he rounded on her for doing such a thing. Out of the corner of my eye, I saw her standing at the door, watching me. When I turned to confront her, she was gone.

CHAPTER FIVE

September slid towards October. School rocked along just like it always did. High school didn't seem that different from junior high to me. I went to class, did my homework and shied around the boys, who had not forgotten my accident on the stairs and twitted me about it every chance they got. I didn't know if I would ever live that down. They made my life pure misery. I did everything I could to avoid them, but it wasn't always possible.

Except for music class, which I loved, school was mostly something to be endured. I sailed through English and struggled through algebra. If it hadn't been for Patty's help, I wouldn't have made it at all. I just couldn't wrap my brain around the concept of things always being worked the same way, and finding x and y confused me in ways I couldn't even begin to describe. I would work a problem in a way that made perfect sense to me and then find out it was wrong because I hadn't followed the steps. Patty would laugh at me and help me fix my mistakes. I would have felt bad about having to have her help all the time, but she was just as hopeless at English as I was at algebra. I figured that made us even.

Over the past weeks, we'd become really close friends: the kind a person could tell her heart's secrets to and know that it would never be turned on her or told to anyone else. It was Patty I turned to when I felt I couldn't endure another moment at home. There were a lot of those times. Patty was always there to listen, though she didn't have much advice to give. She would pat me on the shoulder and then begin to tease me until I laughed. Sometimes we even got to go for a Coke when she could arrange for her dad to bring me home. Daddy wasn't wild about my running around, but Grace, to her credit, had insisted that I was a young girl and needed to have a little fun when Daddy reminded me that I had things to do at home.

Because I had rebuffed her the first time, Grace hadn't made the offer of a beauty shop visit and twin set again. In fact, she didn't speak to me unless she had to. She was leaving me alone all right. I pretty much followed her lead. I did the things I was supposed to do to help her, and then I fled to my room to do homework or went tramping down by the creek to avoid her. The creek was one of the few things that hadn't changed in my life. The green of summer would soon be displaced by the gold of autumn leaves, but for now there was still warmth and sunlight that soothed me in my unhappiness at the way things were.

Although I avoided her, she and the little kids were thick as molasses and did everything together these days. I reminded myself that I didn't *want* to be close to her, but seeing them together made me feel left out and lonely. Sometimes I came in and she and the twins would be making cookies together, with her laughing at some nonsense they had said—not that I liked the twins any better than I had before *she* came on the scene, but, every now and then, I felt this twinge of jealousy. They were so wrapped up in her they forgot to annoy me. I should have been happy I guess. Life was a lot quieter, and I didn't have nearly as many things to do around the house as I once did. The trouble was, it seemed a lot lonelier because everyone else seemed to be happy, and I was alone in my misery. Sometimes I felt I was the only one who missed Mama. I particularly hated the closeness she and Daddy seemed to have found together. She made him laugh and the looks he turned toward her were tender. It twisted me up inside. She and Daddy were so happy together that I couldn't stand it. How could he be so happy? It wasn't that long since Mama had passed. Well, if he could forget, I couldn't. And wouldn't, I vowed. I'd never accept her in place of Mama. She and Daddy could just forget about that.

We were well into the last week of September. The hot weather had hung on and stayed in the nineties. I'd come home every day from school with my hair plastered to my neck with sweat, wishing I had taken her up on that offer of a haircut. A haircut sounded nice, but Daddy would have yelled blue murder if I cut my hair off. Today I gathered it up in a tail on the top of my head and fished out some hairpins, fussing at myself because not only had I missed an opportunity to have the latest do, but also I had missed the opportunity to cause her some grief with Daddy. I changed my clothes and fished out an old pair of shorts and a shirt that was faded and soft with many washings and nearly too small for me. I was surprised. The last time I had put this shirt on, it had fit. I hadn't grown any curves yet, as the other girls had, but I was taller. It looked as if I never was going to grow anything approaching a curve. I was still undersized and scrawny, even if my clothes said I had grown. I grimaced at the image in the mirror.

I'd gotten done with the chores early today and I was going down to the creek. I planned to kick off my shoes and wade. The thought of the cool water was heaven, even if the creek tended to be a bit muddy. The shirt and old shorts really didn't matter where I was heading. The red mud stained everything a dirty rust color and there wasn't enough bleach in the world to get it out of white clothes. It wouldn't matter if I "slipped" and fell in and got my clothes muddy. Daddy didn't like me playing in the creek by myself, but I did it anyway. Its lure was irresistible.

I was halfway down to the creek when I heard Johnny behind me.

"Where ya goin'?" He yelled, pelting up the path behind me.

"Isn't it obvious?" I gritted my teeth. I was hot and in a bad mood and the last thing I wanted was a tag-along. Johnny never could take a hint though.

"I want to go!"

"I want to be by myself for a while!"

"You've always got to be by yourself. Why can't I go with you this once?" He whined. He turned around and started scuffing his way back toward the house. A little way down the path he turned. "You don't want to be around ANY of us anymore. You don't even want to be my sister! Well you just go on and be by yourself. You just see if I care!" This time he stomped away, leaving me stunned. It had never occurred to me that Johnny, of all people, might want my company.

I stood there for a minute, feeling guilty, and then called after him, "Oh, all right. Come on then."

He stopped mid-stomp, turned, and gave me a smile that nearly took my breath away. I hadn't seen him smile like that in a while. Johnny had a smile that could light up the whole world. It melted some of the ice I had so carefully kept built up around my heart. "Come on! I'll race you!" I yelled and took off down the path. He was past me and beyond before I could get very far.

"Man, you're getting fast!" I puffed when I finally caught up with him. I shoved the hair that had come falling out of the ponytail out of my eyes. "You may even be a track star one day!" I could see him just sort of swell up like a balloon at that. I didn't praise him every day—mostly because I didn't want him to start getting the big head and get more insufferable than he already was.

"Nah," he said modestly. "I'm only good at beating girls!" He grinned and ducked the cuff I directed at him. "Last one in is a rotten egg!" He launched himself into the water and sent a wave of water hurling up on the bank at me. He wasn't supposed to be in the creek either, but, being Johnny, he usually did what he wanted, even if he got in trouble for it. Unlike me, he didn't make excuses for his misbehaviors. He just did them.

"I'm gonna get you for that one!" I landed in the water with a large splash and we spent several satisfying minutes trying to get each other really wet. We splashed for quite a while and then crawled out and let ourselves dry in the sun. I relaxed, back against a tree, and watched the sparrows flitting back and forth through the branches of the gnarled old trees on the bank of the creek, enjoying the late summer afternoon. The creek, muddy and stained with the clay from its banks, meandered lazily out of sight on its way to eventually join the Washita River. Locusts were singing their last, whirring, Indian Summer song, and now and again, I could hear the plop as a fat frog took its turn at splashing or a fish jumped out of the water after a dragonfly. I closed my eyes and allowed my thoughts to drift aimlessly, only to sneeze because Johnny had found a long grass straw and was tickling my nose with it.

"For crying out loud! Quit it!" I sat up and glared at him, grabbing at the straw, which he yanked out of my reach, only to reach forward and tickle me with it again.

"Stop it, I said!"

"Okay. Okay. I just wanted to play! He made his ugliest face at me.

"Johnny! Can't you ever leave off being a pest?"

"Nope!" He expertly dodged the slap I aimed at him and grinned. I stuck my tongue out at him and made my ugliest face back, and we both laughed. Every now and then, Johnny was tolerable, even if he was a pest.

A sudden. hard breeze sprang up and a shadow passed over where we were sitting. I looked up and didn't like what I saw. While we had splashed in the creek, a large, boiling storm cloud had been building to the southwest and it looked as though it were moving our way fast. It lowered on the horizon, black and menacing, like a strange evil creature waiting to pounce. From the depths of its being issued a rumble of thunder.

I hated storms. They scared me to death. That was an improvement over the terror I had felt when I was little. I had been paralyzed with fear then. Now, I moved quickly.

"We'd better get home, Johnny. It looks like it's going to storm." I gathered up my shoes and slipped them on, heedless of filling them with mud from my dirty feet. "Hurry!" Already leaves and twigs were beginning to swirl along the way and eddies of dust danced wildly as we raced towards home. A flash of lightning streaked across the sky followed quickly by crack of thunder that was too close for comfort. "Looks like we're in for it! Run!"

Johnny, for once, didn't argue. He didn't like

storms either. He and I pelted up the path to the house as the first drops of cold rain began to fall. We got to the house about the time the storm did. Sheets of rain and gusts of wind announced the storm's arrival. The storm had hit so fast that Grace had had no time to gather in the sheets she had hung out, and they twisted and writhed in the gale like tormented souls, wrapping themselves around and around the clothesline or breaking free altogether to go sailing across the lawn and twine themselves in the trees at its edge. None of us at that point were exactly worrying about sheets. We were more worried about ourselves.

You'd think, growing up in Oklahoma, we'd take it all in stride. We had storms all the time. We also had a nice stout cellar that opened up outside by the porch. Thank goodness, Daddy had come in from work. After a look at the cloud, he helped herd all of us into it. He hadn't seen a funnel, but it was better to be safe than sorry. He and Gramps Gibson had dug that cellar and poured the concrete the summer before Gramps had passed. It was a large one, roomy enough to hold a bed and a herd of kids and it was closed with a heavy door made of stout two-by-fours. I'd tried to lift it once. Even with the counterweight to help, it was beyond me. We often spent entire nights in that cellar when it was stormy. From the looks of the sky, we might be doing that once again.

Once we were below he conducted a head count, lit the kerosene lantern, and closed the door. Johnny and I were shivering in our wet clothes, having been soaked as we pelted to the house.

Lanie and Janie were wailing about their dolls.
That set the two little ones to crying too and Grace
had all she could do to quiet them. Georgie was
worried about his cat, and although he didn't cry
like the littler ones, I could tell he wanted to. I
wasn't far from it myself—there was nothing like
being hemmed up somewhere with a bunch of
squalling kids. I gathered Georgie into my lap, and
hugged him.

"Your kitty will be all right, Georgie. She's a
smart kitty! She'll know where to hide!" I said to
make him feel better and hugged him close,
resting my chin on the top of his tousled head.
Georgie loved Miss Kitty, his calico cat, fiercely,
and I had overheard him talking to her when he
wouldn't talk to anyone else. He would hug the
purring cat closely to him and whisper in her ear.
The cat would purr and gaze at him intently, as
though she understood every word he said.
Georgie was kind of like a cat himself, I thought.

"You really think so?" He asked.

"Sure I do!" Actually, I didn't. I wouldn't
want to be a cat and caught in this, but then cats
could get in places people couldn't. Just about that
moment all the twin's caterwauling ceased and in
the sudden silence we heard a faint mew. That not-
so-stupid cat had zipped down the stairs ahead of
us and was crouching under the bench, looking
pleased with herself. We hadn't heard her in all
the commotion. "See!" I said. "There she is."

Georgie bounded off my lap with a cry of
delight and scooped her up. We could hear her
purring loudly. I wanted to cheer. Daddy, however,

did not feel that way.

"We don't need a cat in here. She'll draw lightning," Daddy said sternly. All the light in Georgie's face snuffed out, just like a candle. I couldn't stand it.

"You just put her out and break Georgie's heart!" I lifted my chin at Daddy and glared. Daddy glared back. He hated sassing. I'd probably pay for it, but if keeping the cat safe could bring back a smile to Georgie's face, it was worth it.

"That's just about enough out of you," he said and would have said more, but at that moment there was a great crack of lightning and the smell of something burning. The little girls screamed and cowered back, causing a fresh outburst from Bobby and Joey. Grace had all she could do to quiet them. The cat streaked under the bed, and Georgie dived after her. Johnny's face, lit up by the lantern, was a study in alarm.

Daddy raised the lid of the cellar just enough to see what had been hit. A spray of cold, wet rain hit him in the face and he drew back, wiping his face. "I think that was the tree at the end of the drive, but I can't tell." *See,* I wanted to tell him. *That was at the end of the drive. The cat didn't do it.* His words were followed by the sound of hail pummeling the cellar door. "Haven't seen such a storm in a long time. Hope we have a house left."

We were in the cellar for quite a while. The little ones huddled around Grace, who hummed softly to them. Johnny and Georgie leaned up against me with Georgie cuddling the now calmer cat, who reached up a soft, white paw and patted Georgie's face before settling down to purr herself to sleep in his arms. I leaned back against the wall and closed my eyes, remembering how Mama used to come and sit with me when I was little and so terrified of storms. I remembered the stories she told me of the elves bowling and how her Papa had told her it was a potato wagon rumbling across the sky. Somehow I had been less afraid then. Mama had made everything seem safer. I wished she were here now. Shivering, I drew an old patchwork quilt over the boys and me and settled down to wait until Daddy gave the all-clear.

We finally emerged into a twilight calm. In the west, the sun glowed beneath the edge of the dark clouds, casting a butter yellow light on the litter of sheets and broken tree branches that lay everywhere. The house seemed all right, but Daddy had been right about the tree. One of the old elms that lined the drive was down. It was split down the middle.

"Golly! Would ya look at that!" Johnny breathed. He and I stood there taking it in.

"Annie, I need yours and Johnny's help in gathering those sheets up and I'm going to get these little ones to bed." Grace said. "Then I think you better have a bath. You too, Johnny." She eyed our mud-stained clothes pointedly.

"Shoulda stood out in the rain," he muttered as we began to gather up sheets from where they were flung by the storm. *Another afternoon of washing,* I grumped to myself. Johnny tried to slip off after we were finished, but I grabbed him. He was at the age when any contact with water besides that done in swimming was to be avoided. We usually had to hunt him at bath time and I'd had to take a washcloth to his ears and face and neck more than once after he'd had one. The wash cloth usually got what he had missed and came away dark with dirt. Grabbing his shoulders, I pointed him in the direction of the bathroom. If he didn't take his first, we'd have a time finding him.

"Don't use all the hot water!" I yelled at Johnny as I followed Grace up the stairs, furious that she had spoken to me as though I were ten. Of course, he did use all the hot water and that put me in a worse mood, especially after I had to employ the washcloth once more to him, and I had to take a cold bath. Then we had to make the beds. I thought sadly of the once clean sheets that would have to be washed again. *More work.*

Grace asked me to help her get the babies to bed. Still aggravated at Johnny, I fumed through helping Grace to get the babies settled and, and impatiently yanked a comb through the twins' tangled mops, causing them to yell in protest.

"You don't have to be so rough, Annie," Grace said mildly. "Leave them some hair."

"Leave me alone. I know what I'm doing."

"Do you?" Those pale gray eyes were boring into me and the tone was disapproving.

"Yes I do!" I snapped back as I took a last lick at Janie's head with a yank that caused her to let out a yelp.

"You're MEAAANNNNN!" she wailed. "You're always mean! I hate you!" she wailed.

"Shut up you little brat!"

"Annie, that's enough." Grace's tone was sharp—sharper than she had ever used to me before. "She's right you know. You go out of your way to be unpleasant to these girls."

"Oh yeah. I forgot. They're your little angels. They can do no wrong,"

Grace's face went white with fury, "Listen here. I've put up with your rudeness ever since I married your Dad. Being rude to me is one thing. I will not allow you to be mean to your sisters. I think you'd better leave this room before I say things I'll regret."

"Like what? I put my hands on my hips and dared her to do something. I'd been waiting for this for a long time. "You really think I care what you think? You tried to take my Mama's place and you never will with me. You walk right in and take over and put her stuff away and you never even think about how anyone feels. You've even turned my Daddy against me. I can't even do anything right any more. It's all your fault," I hissed.

"Okay, little lady. I have some things to say too. I'm not putting up with any more of your moods or your selfish, hateful ways. I'm not trying to take the place of your Mama, but there are things I have to do to take care of her children. One of those is to protect them. Apparently she didn't teach you how to treat them."

"You shut up about my Mama. You don't

know anything!" I screamed, clenching and unclenching my fists. The twins hunkered down in the beds, whimpering.

"What doesn't she know?" Daddy's voice, deadly quiet from the doorway brought me up short. I hung my head sullenly and didn't answer.

"*What* doesn't she know?" His voice came sharper. "No, Grace, be quiet. I heard it all. Annie, if I ever hear of you mistreating your sisters or sassing Grace again, I'll make you regret it. I've had it with your rudeness and selfishness too."

"But, she..." I started to answer, but he wasn't through.

"No, you be quiet. I'm having my say, and you better not push me to do more. You've been parading around here like the queen of the May, nursing your grudges and making life miserable for everyone around here. I'm tired of it. Your mother is *dead* and nothing is going to change that. I'm still alive. I had to go on with my life and Grace was who I chose to spend it with. I will not have you sassing her and punishing her because I chose her. I don't want to hear any more tonight. You sleep downstairs tonight and stay away from your sisters."

Daddy's words were hurled at me like the hailstones that had fallen on our cellar door, and each word hurt as it hit. I ran out of the room and headed for the bathroom and slammed the door and locked it.

It was clear he didn't love me anymore. I leaned against the door and let the tears run down my face. All he cared about was Grace and the other kids. He didn't care anything about how I felt; that was plain. My heart hurt. I clenched a fist over it and drew a deep, shuddering breath. He wasn't the only one who couldn't stand things anymore.

Daddy didn't try to coax or threaten me to get me out of the bathroom even though Johnny complained loudly that he needed in there. I slipped out and let him in, and then slipped back in again. I stayed in there, feeling as though the world had ended, until the house was quiet and then went quietly down the hall to the stairs, intending to slip out into the night air. When I heard their voices from the bedroom. I stopped and then put my ear to the door.

"Honestly, Thomas. I don't know what I did so wrong," Grace was saying. "I've honestly tried. I shouldn't have lost it with her." Her voice was tired-sounding and sad.

"Yes, you should have. She's been bad to you all along. I don't know how you take it like you do."

"I take it because I know she was hurting, but I just can't put up with her being mean like that to the little girls."

"I don't think she's going to change her ways any time soon. Are you sure you can deal with her? I'm fixing to take her down a peg or two."

"I'll do my best."

"Maybe I should send her to live with her Aunt May. Eve loves her. It'd be a lot more peaceful around here."

I sucked in a breath.

"Oh, Thomas, send her away?"

"You got any better ideas? I don't know what to do with her anymore. I'm telling you, Grace, I don't know what happened to that sweet little girl I had."

I'm still here Daddy, I mouthed silently. *I just can't get around Grace to you.*

"It's the age she is, and losing her mother too. I wasn't sweetness and light either at her age," she admitted with a rueful chuckle.

"Now I'll never believe that! Come on, turn out the light and let's get to bed. Storms are over for now, outside and inside. We'll talk about it in the morning after we all calm down." The light winked out under the door.

I stood there for a little while in the darkness of the hallway and then tiptoed to the room where the twins had finally gone to sleep. The clouds outside had cleared away, and the moon was shining. A beam of moonlight shone on their sleeping faces. Looking at them, I felt a stirring of remorse. Asleep they looked like innocent angels. They thought I was mean. I shouldn't have been mean to them. It wasn't their fault that I was so mad at the world. They were little.

Ignoring Daddy's command to go downstairs to sleep and stay away from them, I crawled into bed between them. Janie stirred and sleepily snuggled down into my arms, Lanie turned over and threw one arm over me. I lay there, sandwiched between them, and stared into the darkness. I was still awake when Daddy came in later to check on them, but I shut my eyes and pretended to be asleep. I heard him sigh and felt his hand stroke my hair gently, although I didn't respond. He moved quietly to the door and went on out. My dark thoughts and resentments followed him into the hallway.

CHAPTER SIX

"Ann Marie Gibson, you and Patty stop talking and pay attention!" Mrs. Oldham glared at us over her half glasses. She was everyone's image of an English teacher, down to the gray bun and the tan walking shoes, and she was very, very fond of Shakespeare, who wrote in a foreign language to most of us. She had been dragging us through Shakespeare's *Romeo and Juliet* for a week now. Even though I was good at reading, I was having a hard time understanding all those strange words he used, and Patty was absolutely lost. I had trouble keeping a straight face when Mrs. Oldham was reading the balcony scene.

To her credit, she was trying to make it interesting, using two different voices, which was only moderately successful. Some of the kids were staring off into space and Sally Moore was staring boredly at her nails, which she had painted a bright scarlet. I tried to imagine Sally on the balcony as Juliet but my imagination failed me. It did, however, tickle my sense of humor. I could just imagine her nasal twang delivering the lines. I stifled a giggle and tried to look innocent, when Mrs. Oldham looked up.

Patty looked over at me, rolled her eyes, and grinned. I grinned back and shot a look at Mrs. Oldham to see if she was watching us. Deep once more in the throes of *Romeo and Juliet,* she missed our little exchange. When the bell rang a few minutes later, I thankfully gathered up my books and scurried out the door. Patty bounced behind me.

"Ohmigosh! That was just too boring!" she sighed. "I just can't get into that stuff."

"I know, but you've got to stop making faces or we'll be in deep trouble!" I said.

"Well you were the one laughing! What were you laughing about? That stuff is the most boring stuff ever!" she retorted as we hurried along the hallway and up the stairs. The girls in the popular crowd all waved cheerful hellos to Patty, totally ignoring me, except for Sally, who looked at me as if I were a disgusting specimen under the microscope that we were using in biology class.

She had made it her personal mission to make my life miserable, and made sure to subvert any friendly overtures that any of the other girls might make. I don't know why I had ever considered her a friend. She certainly didn't fit that description now. I didn't mind the girls' liking Patty, but I wished they wouldn't be so unaccepting of me. I figured Sally had told them how hateful I was, after I had told her off about being nosy about my home life, and turned them against me. Maybe they just didn't want someone who wasn't stylish hanging around with their crowd.

I wished the boys had ignored me like the

girls did. They didn't. They wolf-whistled and cat-called and made their usual rude remarks about wanting a date with me. They had tried that with Patty, but she just batted her eyelashes at them and gave them as good as they gave. I wished I was as good with a comeback line as she was, but I wasn't. Mostly I would have just liked to fly into the crowd of boys and deal with them as I dealt with Johnny, but it wasn't ladylike, and it would just add to their reasons to persecute me. I gritted my teeth, put my chin in the air, and sailed past the crowd of boys into the music room. Surely they had better things to do than harass me.

I slid into a seat in the first row. Patty came in a few minutes later, just before the tardy bell. Sally and her crowd flounced in and sat down in the second row. They whispered behind their hands and giggled. I was obviously a topic of their conversation. *Forget them!* I told myself, and slid over one chair so Patty could sit down.

I opened my folder of music and made a big business of getting out the first piece of sheet music. I looked forward to this class all day. It was the one place, besides the place at the creek, where I felt content. It was a big, airy room with a bank of windows on the west and the afternoon light spilled like a benediction across the scuffed floors, and scattered music on the battered piano we used to practice. I felt totally at home here.

I liked to sing, and Mrs. Colman told me I had a really nice voice. She had even offered to give me voice lessons. Unfortunately, I didn't have time. There was too much to do at home, I told her. She gave me a regretful nod and didn't offer again. I think she was as disappointed as I was. Anyway, something was wrong with Grace.

Grace had been getting paler and thinner lately. Sometimes I could hear her retching, although she never complained. We still weren't speaking much. We were being very carefully polite. I was polite because of what Daddy had said to her about sending me away, although he didn't know I had overheard him. She was polite in that way grownups have of being polite when they really don't want you around but don't want to outright say so. It was all very poisonous in a sickly sweet way. After losing her temper, she seemed determined not to let me get to her again, although I tried. She wasn't that way with the other kids though. With them, she had no need to tiptoe around to avoid hurt feelings or an all-out confrontation.

Sometimes, watching her and the little kids play and joke, I would almost wish things were different, but then I'd think of Mama and how Grace took her place, and I'd feel all mad and sad again. I'd go up to my room and shut the door to keep from storming at her. I did make sure that I hit that lower step real hard every morning, just to irritate her. It was the least I could do. She bore it with stoic silence.

Patty had been nagging at me for weeks to come to my house. I had always put her off. I didn't know how she and Grace would hit it off. Our house, in spite of the improvements Grace had been working on, was really shabby too. Eight kids can wreak a lot of wear on a place. Patty's was always clean and uncluttered, and the things she and her family had looked brand new.

I finally told Patty she could come over after she pitched a fit at me about it. I wasn't happy about taking her out there though. It gave me ulcers just thinking about it. Today was "Patty Day." She was coming over after school. Grace had excused me from my chores for the afternoon, so I could entertain Patty. I dreaded it. What if my house wasn't good enough? I didn't want her to pity me.

The joy of singing put off the dread for a little while. I was able to lose myself in learning the intricate melody Mrs. Colman had selected for us to learn that day. All too soon, the hour was over, and I had to take Patty home for what I hoped wouldn't be a disaster.

Grace and the younger kids were in the kitchen when we got there. She was putting a pan of ginger cookies in the oven. A plateful of newly baked and cooled cookies was on the table, and the kids were happily stuffing themselves. The smell made my mouth water. Patty, being Patty, went into raptures.

"Yum! Those smell really good, Mrs. Gibson! Could I have one?"

"Surely!" Grace smiled and offered her the plate. She had a streak of flour on her nose and she was flushed from the heat of the oven. "Would you like some milk to wash them down with?"

I opened my mouth to refuse but was

forestalled by Patty's enthusiastic "Yes!" Grace got out two glasses from the cabinet and filled them with milk. I sat down at the end of the table and sipped the cold milk, watching Patty make herself at home. The shabbiness of our house did not seem to bother her. Not once did she look around as if she were judging where we lived. She was more focused on us.

She plopped herself down among my brothers and sisters and proceeded to tease and clown until they were giggling wildly. Grace leaned against the refrigerator and joined in. I was the only one who wasn't laughing. As soon as I could, I grabbed Patty and dragged her upstairs to my room. She followed me up the stairs, still chuckling under her breath.

"Your brothers and sisters are *so* cute!" she crowed, throwing herself across my bed.

"You don't have to live with them!" I retorted and felt sorry immediately because her face went sad.

"No, no, I don't." she said quietly. "I wish I could. It's lonely at my house."

This wasn't like Patty at all. I realized with a guilty start that I really didn't know how Patty felt about anything. I'd been too busy dwelling on my troubles to think whether or not she might have any herself. She wasn't one to parade hers either.

"Gee, I'm sorry, Patty, but I'll rent you some if you want!" I said in an attempt to lighten her mood.

"Good! I'll take all of them!" she replied. "It looks like that stepmother of yours could use the rest!"

"Who? Grace?"

"Yeah. I've never seen anyone so pale in all my life!"

"That's just Grace!" I replied. Why was she so concerned over my not-so-dearly-beloved stepmother?

"No, there's something wrong, I think." Patty said seriously. "I think she's sick or something."

"Well, she HAS been throwing up in the mornings...wait!" I was stopped cold by a sudden thought. Mama had been sick like that when she... "Oh no!" I cried and plopped down on the side of the bed.

"What?" Patty rolled over and sat up. "What is it?"

"I hope I'm wrong!" I said miserably. "I don't want to talk about it right now."

"All right," Patty said doubtfully. I could see she wanted to ask me a thousand questions, but I changed the subject by jumping up and asking her if she wanted to see my secret place down by the river, and dragging her out the door. We spent the rest of the afternoon there until she had to go home. We giggled about Mark Jones, the cutest boy in the senior class, and talked about school, but we did not talk about Grace's mysterious illness and what I thought it was. I was relieved when she finally went home.

Grace was in the kitchen peeling potatoes when I came in. The radio was on and she didn't hear me enter. I stood there in the doorway looking at her. She did look awfully pale and tired.

I felt uncomfortable. I hadn't noticed. I was embarrassed that Patty had to tell me. I didn't like her but I didn't want to seem like a total monster either.

"Grace?" I said tentatively. "Are you sick?"

She jumped.

"Oh! You startled me!"

"I'm sorry. Patty said you didn't look well, so I thought I'd ask."

The look of surprise on her face was replaced by a wary expression.

"It's nothing, Annie," she wiped her forehead with the back of her hand. "It will pass."

"Uh, yeah, I'm sure it will," I said. "Uh...why don't you go lie down or something. I'll finish these."

She shot me a look of pure astonishment at my offer, then caught herself and smiled. For an instant, she was almost pretty. "Why, thank you! I *am* feeling tired. I'll just lie down for a moment..."

"Sure. Sure...you go on. I'll get these peeled and on the stove. Mashed or fried?" I took the knife from her and busied myself at peeling a potato.

"I promised the twins we'd have smashed potatoes this evening, so mashed will do fine. The pot's ready on the stove."

"I'll get them ready. You go lie down or something," I said, waving the potato in the general direction of the living room. "I'll call you when the potatoes are done," I said hastily to keep her from saying anything else. I was already regretting my offer. There was a small mountain of potatoes on the tabletop. It would probably take forever.

With a final, grateful look that made me squirm inside, Grace drifted into the living room and lay down on the couch. I kept on peeling potatoes. I blinked back tears and swallowed the big knot that came into my throat. The baby would be about five months old now, I thought, and Mama would be laughing and playing with her while I peeled potatoes. I pulled myself out of that dream with a jerk.

Stop it! I told myself. That won't bring her back and all you're doing is making it worse on yourself. The tears I had held back for so long began to brim over and spill down my face. One dripped off the end of my nose and I wiped it off with a potato-smudged finger. At that moment Johnny came skidding into the room. He stopped dead when he saw my woebegone face and stared.

"Gee, Annie! You in trouble *again?*"

"No, I'm not. I just got something in my eye, all right?"

"In both eyes?"

"Look, pest. Go away and leave me alone!" Count on Johnny to snap me out of it and aggravate me to death in the bargain.

"I was just asking. You don't have to be so hateful!" He stuck his tongue out at me and caught the potato I threw at him.

"Get out of here!"

"I'm going! I'm going!" He headed out the door, stopping to give me a raspberry over his shoulder.

All of a sudden, I was laughing—laughing so hard I nearly doubled over. To this day, I don't know why I was laughing. Maybe, it was better than crying. Anyway, once I stopped laughing I felt a little better. I finished the potato peeling and got the potatoes cooking. Then I went to wake up Grace. I paused at the living room door, watching her sleep for a moment.

She was lying on her side, both hands tucked under her cheek. Asleep, she didn't look much older than I was. An unaccustomed sense of pity moved me. She *did* look worn out. The feeling warred with the old resentment, causing my stomach to begin churning. I didn't want to feel anything for her. I went over to the couch and shook her shoulder.

"Grace, you said to wake you up," I said loudly.

"Oh! Mmmph!" Her eyes flew open and she sat up suddenly, only to collapse on the couch again.

"Come on, Grace. Wake up!"

"Dizzy," she murmured and sat up more slowly this time. "Sorry. Did you get the potatoes peeled?"

"Yes, I did. And they're already on the stove, cooking."

"Thank you, Annie!" She smiled sleepily at me and sat up and smoothed her hair. "I must have dozed off."

"Grace? Can I ask you something?"

She was instantly on guard. "What?"

"Are you expecting?"

For a minute, she didn't say anything. She was no doubt wondering if she ought to say anything to me, forgetting that I'd been through this eight times with Mama. Then she stood up and went and looked out the window. She stood there a moment, twisting her hands, and then turned to me.

"Yes. Yes, I am. How did you guess?"

Oh come on now, I thought, but I only said, "Mama used to look pale and tired and get dizzy like you do when she was in the family way."

"Oh...Oh! I guess I'm not good at keeping secrets, huh?" She was searching my face to try to figure out how I was going to react. "I really didn't want to tell anyone yet. I haven't even told your Daddy."

"You haven't?" I was totally taken aback. "Why?"

"I wanted to be sure, and well, the right time just hasn't come up yet," She came over, started to take my hands, thought better of it, and settled for peering earnestly into my face. "You won't tell him before I get a chance to will you?"

A small voice inside me whispered nastily, "Wouldn't I just like to!" I stood there a minute or two and then said grudgingly, "I guess not."

"Thank you! I don't know how he'll take it."

Another baby. I didn't know how to take it either.

It turned out he was as happy as a man could be. You'd have thought it was his first instead of his ninth (if you counted the one that died). She told him after supper. He let out a whoop, jumped out of his chair and swung Grace around. The other kids came running from the four corners of the house to see what all the commotion was about. They joined in and there was general pandemonium for at least ten minutes. I stood in the doorway and watched them, wishing I could feel as joyful.

Maybe that's the curse of being older, I thought. *I'm not a kid anymore. I can look ahead and see all the problems coming.* I scooped up Joey when he came toddling toward me and nuzzled his neck to hide my face. If I showed a sad face, they'd resent it of course. Joey giggled and drew back and pushed my cheeks together with his pudgy, little fists. I made a great show of playing with him. As soon as I could, I escaped upstairs and threw myself across the bed. I guess I drifted off to sleep because the next thing I know, I had the twins straddled across my back and they were bouncing up and down.

"Ow! Get off!" I yelled and rolled over, depositing them unceremoniously on the bed. "Go away! Can't a girl get any peace around here?"

"We want to play piggy back ride," they whined, and launched themselves at me again. As I fended them off, I thought, Great! Another kid to drive me crazy.

"Go away you little beasts!"

"Daddddddyyyyyyyy!" Lanie wailed. "Annie's calling us naaaames." She flung herself at me again and tried to pummel me with her fists. I held her at arm's length so that she couldn't hurt me. Janie, in the meantime, had grabbed me around the neck.

"Daddy! Make them get out of my room. I was minding my own business!" I shouted, determined that for once, they'd get theirs.

I heard him coming up the steps, skipping every tread. He stopped at the door and watched for a second, then waded in and pulled the twins away.

"You two stop it this minute! Go downstairs! Now!"

The twins shot him mutinous glances but knew better than to talk back. They slunk downstairs, probably to annoy someone else. I hoped it was Johnny rather than Georgie. Georgie was no match for them. Johnny would make no bones about putting them in line.

Daddy turned back to me.

"I wondered where you had gotten to," he said. "You okay?"

"I'm fine," I yawned elaborately. "I was just tired. Oh shoot! What time is it? I have an essay to do." I really didn't want to have a heart to heart talk with Daddy just then. I couldn't tell him how I was feeling. I didn't think he would understand.

"Uh, well, you'd better get after it then," he said after a moment. I guess he was as ill at ease as I was. He stumped out of the room and down the stairs. I stared after him, wishing we could talk like we used to, but how could I tell him all the things I was feeling when I hadn't sorted them out myself, and when he was sure to be angry at some of the things I felt. Sighing, I took out my book bag, dragged my notebook out, rubbed my eyes, and began to write.

CHAPTER SEVEN

It was a while before I let Patty in on the new baby to come. I finally told her the news on the way to music class one day. She got all round-eyed and stopped suddenly in her tracks, causing a pair of sophomores to crash into her from behind. Shooting us dirty looks, they went on up the hallway while Patty regarded me with delight, oblivious to the mayhem she had caused.

"Wow! Aren't you lucky!" she crowed.

"How's that? It doesn't feel real lucky to me," I grumped.

Her face became incredulous and she said seriously, "All those brothers and sisters! And I don't have *any*. I'd love just to have even one. It's kind of lonely at my house."

I was startled. I hadn't thought of a new baby's being a blessing. Heaven knew Johnny and the others sometimes didn't feel much like a blessing to me. I thought of Patty's house, kept in shining order with no evidence of busy little hands at work. It was quiet—maybe too quiet. It hadn't occurred to me to think I was blessed. All of a sudden I felt sorry for her.

"Hey listen!" I said to lighten the moment.

"I'll let you have Johnny!"

"Nope! I want one of the others! You can keep *him*!" The wistful look left her face and she laughed as we started off down the hall. "Did you get your math homework done last night?"

"No, I just don't get that stuff. It's way too hard."

"No it isn't. It's just figuring out what x is."

"That's the problem. I'm not even sure what x means!"

"You expect me to believe that? You make A's in English!"

"Yeah, but math is a whole other language," I shot at her over my shoulder as we entered the music room. Mrs. Colman had told me that I was to have a solo for the next program. Today we were practicing it and I was a little nervous, but knowing that I had a solo to learn and learning it took my mind off the situation at home for a while. What were people going to say when word got around about the baby coming? I could hear the snickers and snide remarks coming my way. "Eight kids, wasn't that enough? Another one?" or "They didn't wait long to produce another." Yes, that was going to cause more than a few comments, I was sure. I prayed that the blessing Patty and I had talked about wouldn't be twins!

Patty and I sat down in the first row of the soprano section next to Rosie Carlisle. Rosie was nice, but she had a tendency to sing off-key. I let Patty sit beside her and took the seat next to Patty as the tardy bell rang and Mrs. Colman tapped on her music stand for order. I liked Mrs. Colman in spite of her big booming voice and gruff ways. I always knew where I stood with her, and my standing was usually good.

"Well class, are you ready to start rehearsing for our Christmas concert? Susan, will you pass out this music please while we warm up our vocal chords? Sally Moore, sit up straight! Lucy Trent, turn around and quit talking. Everyone sing!"

I took the sheet music from Susan, who was moving officiously down the rows, and groaned inwardly. *"Mary Had a Baby"*— *"make that Grace Had a Baby."* I grimaced at the thought.

I managed to get through the song without substituting Grace for Mary, and then Mrs. Colman had us sing through the song I was to sing, a version of "Silent Night" with a special solo at the end. When it was time for me to sing it, I opened my mouth and let the sound pour out of me. When I sang, for that moment, I wasn't plain old Anne Marie anymore. I was one with the music. I was it, and it was me. The first time people heard me sing, it tended to stop them dead in their tracks because the last thing they expected to come out of my mouth was any sound they described as lovely. It never failed to surprise me, either. Mrs. Colman said it was because I put my heart and soul into it. I guess I did.

I sat back down amid a general hubbub once the song had finished. The popular girls were eyeing me with a mixture of envy and disbelief, as though an exotic bird had hatched out of a sparrow's egg. Patty leaned over to me and whispered, "That was great!"

"Thanks!" I muttered. No longer singing, I was once more the frizzy haired Annie with the scrawny body in unstylish clothes and too many brothers and sisters and one more on the way.

CHAPTER EIGHT

The door slammed. It was Daddy, coming in with the mail.

"You have a letter," he said, tossing a pale blue envelope with me. "It's from Grandma Jenkins." His face told me what he thought of that.

I caught the letter, tucked it in my shirt and ran up to my room, where I tore it open. I missed Grandma. It was good to hear from her.

> *Dear Annie,*
>
> *I haven't heard from you in a while, so I hope you are doing well. I would like you and Johnny and Georgie to come for a visit one of these weekends before the cold weather comes. I miss you and would like to see you. I hope your Daddy will allow you to come. for a visit if you would like to come.*

A visit! Would I like to come? Yes, I would. I loved to visit Grandma Jenkins, who lived in a lovely two-story house on a tree-shaded street in Clinton. She always spoiled me outrageously when I visited. There were no chores to do, and she always made the visits fun. She said that was what grandmothers were for.

One summer when I was ten, Mama and my brothers and sisters had all gone to visit and we had gone to the large park there. We had ridden the little steam-engine train around the little circle next to the pool. The engineer, a little, thin stooped-shouldered man, had gotten a kick out of blowing the whistle and seeing the excitement that the little ones had as they piled on the train. Johnny had hogged the backward facing seat at the end of the last green metal car and whooped and yelled all the way through the dimly-lit white-stucco tunnel. Grandma saw that we got to ride as much as we wanted, shelling out dimes liberally for train fare.

Afterwards we had explored the park, looking through the chain-link fence at the swimmers in the deep end of the pool and watching them dive and jump off the boards. In the background, the latest music played from the loud speakers while lifeguards with sun cream on their nose sat sentinel on the life-guards' chairs. We had begged to swim, but Mama had told us that we would save that for later. We had to content ourselves with romping on the swing sets and slide, and running around in the amphitheater with its stage and band shell. We got on the stage and sang off-key with Mama and Grandma Jenkins applauding from the front row of stone-tiered seats.

Johnny had decided to try to run down the stone seats and had managed to fall and skin his legs. I had done that more than once myself, I remembered. We had admired the beautiful cannas and played at the playground and then had eaten a picnic lunch. I smiled at the happiness these memories brought me, and then began reading again.

Please ask your daddy if you may come. You can bring Georgie and Johnny too.

It is my hope that he will allow you to come see us. We have a lot to catch up on. There are some little boys down the street who will be good companions for Johnny and Georgie and the neighbors have said they may come and play, and Grandpa has said he can take the boys on an outing so you and I can enjoy some time to ourselves. I look forward to seeing you. If transportation is an issue, Grandpa and I can come and get you and bring you back.

All my love,
Grandma.

I folded the letter carefully and sat there for a moment. *Would* Daddy let us go? After the big fight they had had, I wasn't sure. I wasn't exactly on his good side either. Well, I could ask. All he could do was to say "no." Gathering up my courage, I went in search of him.

He was sitting in the kitchen with Grace, drinking a cup of coffee. They had been laughing together over something. Her face, which had been alight with laughter, quickly became wary when I entered. Daddy patted the chair beside him.

"Come sit down, Annie. What did your Grandma have to say?

I remained standing, ready to take flight if need be. "She wants Georgie, and Johnny and me to come visit."

"She does, does she?" A frown began to gather itself on his face. "She has a nerve."

Grace made a small sound.

He looked at her and back to me.

"I want to go, Daddy. I haven't seen her in ages," I said. "I know Georgie and Johnny want to see her too," I continued hurriedly. "It's only for a weekend."

The frown deepened. "How does she expect to get you back and forth,"

"She said she and Grandpa will come get me."

"I don't like it."

"Daddy, Please?"

"I'll have to think about it," he said curtly. *At least he didn't say, "no," right away,* I thought. He dropped his chin to his chest. I stood there twisting my hands together anxiously until he looked up and told me to run along.

I fled, He got up and closed the kitchen door behind me. I stopped and crept back to the door, putting my ear against it.

"What are you going to do, Thomas?" Grace asked. She was making no particular effort to keep her voice down, thinking I had gone.

"I don't know. I can't stand the woman. She never did approve of my marrying her daughter. I wasn't good enough. Nothing I did was right.

She'll fill their heads with nonsense."

"Perhaps she won't. I don't know how I would act if I were in her place. Anyway, she *is* the children's grandmother."

"Well, you're being real charitable after all she had to say the last time she was here. She wasn't real complimentary about you either."

I heard Grace chuckle. "She doesn't know me very well."

"I can't have her insulting my wife."

"Can you really take her from her grandchildren?"

"I sure want to." I heard him scrape his chair back and the sound of his steps as he paced back and forth. "She had no right to say what she did."

"Thomas, try to put yourself in her place, a bit. Those children are all she has left of Ella. aren't they?"

I heard him sigh. "Yeah."

"Then be the better person and let her see them. Besides, I'm not going to be the reason she doesn't get to see them. What does that serve? It makes me feel terrible, and Annie will hate me more than ever. Send the children to her, Thomas. Let them visit."

There was a silence. After a while, Daddy sighed. "I guess, when you put it that way, I have to. All right. I'll tell Annie they can go and she can write to her grandmother." I heard the scrape of his chair as he stood up and his steps moving towards the door. I raced away and out the front door and sat on the porch steps, my heart beating wildly at nearly being discovered.

"Annie?" He called.

"Out here, Daddy."

He came out on the porch and sat down on the steps next to me.

"I've thought about it. I still don't like it, but Grace seems to think I need to let you go."

"Tell her I said, 'thank you,'" I said stiffly. Grace was right. I would have blamed her if I hadn't gotten to go. It rankled that she had to intercede on my behalf with Daddy, though.

"I will tell you this, young lady. If you come back with a hateful attitude and mistreat Grace in any way because your grandma doesn't like her, you won't get to see the woman again until you're grown." His hand grasped my chin and turned my face to look at him. His eyes gazed into mine fiercely. "Do you hear me?"

"Yes, Daddy," I swallowed. "I promise I'll try to be good."

"Trying isn't good enough. You'd just better act right." He released my chin from his grasp and stood up. "You can write your grandma. You three can go visit weekend after next. She can come and get you and bring you back. I'm not going out of my way for her." He went back into the house.

I stared after him. I was getting to go, but he had put a high price on my going. I knew my Daddy well enough, though, to know he meant what he said. Once he set his mind on something, that was the way it was, and no argument in the world changed his viewpoint. I sighed, and got up to go write to Grandma Jenkins.

She wrote me back that she and Grandpa were delighted that we were getting to visit and that she and Grandpa would be down to pick us up on Friday of the appointed weekend and bring us back on the following Sunday. I told Daddy what she had written and settled down to wait. For me, the time ahead would drag by unmercifully.

Georgie and Johnny were excited about going, although Georgie was anxious about leaving his cat. He really was too attached to that animal, I thought. Grace assured him that she would watch over Miss Kitty and that he should go and have a good time. Johnny, like me, couldn't wait. He nearly drove me crazy with all the pestering about getting to go. I restrained myself from walloping him more than once because I didn't want to lose out on the chance of going. It was hard though because he was such a nuisance.

To give him credit, Johnny was usually pretty good around Grandma. She never let on that anything he did upset her, so the fun of being bad was taken out of it for him. Grandpa usually took him fishing, which he loved, and he was looking forward to that. Georgie was looking forward to it too. He told me one day that he was going to bring Miss Kitty a fish to eat. I shuddered, thinking of the smell, and told him we would find Miss Kitty a can of tuna, since it wasn't practical to bring a fish home in a suitcase.

It was Grandpa's conviction that all young men should know how to fish. He said it was fun and taught them patience. He tried to get me to fish one time, on one of their visits, but I didn't like baiting the hooks or the fish with their staring googly eyes, and I didn't have the patience to sit still. He had finally given up, but I was still his Girl Number One. I had become that when Lanie and Janie were born. He always made a big production of mixing up Girls Number Two and Three, just to hear them fuss at him. The girls were unhappy that they didn't get to go. I told them that it would be their turn next time. I didn't say that I hoped that there *would* be a next time. There was no use upsetting them.

Grandma had also written that she was bringing gifts for the little ones since they couldn't go this time. I made the mistake of telling them, When they weren't whining about not getting to go they were trying to guess what Grandma would bring them. Daddy snorted when I told him about the gifts, and Grace had to tell him to "be good."

The weekend we were to go for a visit was ablaze with colored leaves and sapphire blue skies. I went about school that Friday, humming under my breath. Patty noticed and remarked on it.

"Gee. Annie. I've never seen you so happy since I've known you. What's up?"

"I get to go to my Grandma's house in Clinton. I haven't seen her in forever!"

"That's really great, Annie!" Patty smiled wistfully. "I wish I could go see mine, but she lives so far away." She had told me that her grandma lived in Kansas, in the town where they had lived before moving to Oklahoma.

"It just as well be far away for all I've gotten

to see her. She and Daddy got into it, and he is barely letting me go."

"That stinks. Well I hope you have a really good time while you are up there."

"I should. I'll still have to put up with Johnny though," I told her. She laughed in commiseration.

"Wow, that should be interesting. Is he taking any of those nasty frogs with him?"

Patty had been his latest victim on her last visit. He had dropped a frog in her lap, to her horror and dismay. I had told her that she was now experiencing some of what I had gone through. Once she had gotten over her shock, she had thought it was pretty funny. She told me her Dad had nearly fallen out of his chair laughing.

"I told him he better not! Grandma says they have things planned for them to do, so we'll see," I replied.

That evening, Johnny had bounced impatiently from the door to the window and back again until I fussed at him to stop. It was only an hour's drive from where we lived and we had to wait for Grandpa to get off work, I reminded him. It would take a little while for them to come get us. Georgie sat on the couch, a tote bag containing his clothing beside him, waiting patiently. Grace had made each of the boys and me bags to put their clothes in, since she had discovered we didn't have suitcases. I had thanked her stiffly. I wished I could be as patient as Georgie seemed to be. Although I put on a cool exterior and pretended I was calm, inside I was pacing as impatiently as Johnny.

When they finally got there, it was Grandpa who came to the door. I guess Grandma wanted to avoid any unpleasantness. Grace opened it and smiled welcomingly and invited him in. Daddy, perhaps also wishing to avoid a confrontation, had announced that he would be working late and wouldn't be there when they came. It was up to Grace to smooth things over.

Grandpa stood just inside the door, looking for all the world as if something were going to bite him until Johnny, hurtling down the stairs after a wild search for his comb and toothbrush, whooped and nearly bowled him over with a hug. Georgie wasn't far behind. Grandpa hugged them back, and then untangled himself and turned to me.

"How's Grandpa's girl? Look how pretty you are!"

"Aw, Grandpa," I gave him my own kiss and hug.

"You ready to go?"

"Yes, I am!" I turned to Grace. "Tell Daddy I love him and tell him 'thank you' for letting us go."

"I will. Did you get everything?"

I assured her I had. I didn't know about Johnny and Georgie though. Johnny was busy peering into his bag to see if he had forgotten anything. I had packed their bags myself. Heaven only knew if they had left everything in the bag, since I knew of at least one occasion of Johnny's dumping his out. Apparently he hadn't put the toothbrush or comb back. At least there wasn't a frog in there. I had assured him there would be frogs at the pond where they were going to go fishing.

"We'll have them home Sunday evening about seven. We'll feed them before they come home, so you won't have to wait supper," Grandpa told her. He kissed the little boys and Lanie and Janie, who had come down the stairs and were noisily demanding their presents, assuring them that they would have them on his return and that they would have something really special.

"That will be fine," Grace assured him over the clamor, "Lanie, Janie, let go of your Grandpa. Bobby, come here. You boys have a good time. Johnny, put your toothbrush in your bag or there's no telling where it will end up. Georgie, you have everything you need? Annie, enjoy yourself. I'm glad you got to go," she said as she gathered the smaller ones around her.

"I am too," I picked up my things and headed for the door, with Johnny and Georgie trailing behind me. Grandpa stuck his hand out to be shaken and Grace took it solemnly.

"Thank you," Grandpa said simply.

"You're very welcome," Grace answered. She watched us out the door as we loaded into Grandpa's old Chevy Bel-Air and waved as we pulled out. Grandma fussed over the boys, and we settled in for the trip. I turned and watched my house growing smaller in the distance, then faced forward. I was going to enjoy this weekend, no matter what.

CHAPTER NINE

When we arrived at Grandma and Grandpa's house that evening, we headed for the rooms we usually stayed in when we came. Grandma had decorated a room for me several years ago, saying a young lady needed a room to herself. It wasn't just my room, since I knew my older girl cousins used it when they came to visit, but I called it mine.

I didn't know what she would do when Lanie and Janie got big enough to want rooms of their own, because, although the house was spacious, there weren't enough bedrooms to give each girl one, unless they used the guest bedroom downstairs, or built on. I'm sure the battle of who got a room to herself would be of historic proportions, knowing those two. By the time they needed one, I would be grown though, and I decided that it wasn't my problem right now. For now, the room was mine, and I reveled in the peace and privacy.

I looked around at the small, cozy room with a sigh of satisfaction. The twin bed was covered with a white, fluffy, chenille spread and adorned with ruffled, pink throw pillows. The two, tall, east windows were covered with white roller shades and framed in crisp, white, lace curtains. The dark stained hardwood floor that Grandma carefully kept shined to a high gloss was graced by a hand hooked rag rug perfect for putting my feet on when I crawled out of bed. A soft, floral scent from sachets tucked in the drawers hung invitingly in the air. In the corner was a vanity with a huge, oval mirror and a ruffled skirting. I loved this room. *If I had this at home, and a lock to keep my sisters out, I wouldn't have to drift down by the creek so much,* I thought, as I put my bag in the closet and arranged my brush and comb on the little vanity.

Actually, on this visit, I pretty much had the whole upstairs to myself. Grandma and Grandpa had installed the boys in the downstairs guest bedroom to keep them close by. Down the hall was the room Mama used to stay in. It had been her room since she was a small girl, and continued to be her room whenever she came back for a visit. I didn't know if Grandma Jenkins let anyone stay in there now. I wandered out of my room and stopped at the door of her room, and opened the door. There it was, unchanged from her last visit, awaiting its owner, unused. I shied away from the pain of the thought. Quietly, I closed the door. I wasn't ready to go in there yet.

Daddy hadn't come with us much, I remembered, and we hadn't stayed the night when he came along. He always insisted on going home the same day. When Mama came alone with us children, though, we had always stayed a day or two. Until I was older I had stayed in Mama's room with her. The room that Grandma had fixed up for me had been one of Mama's sister's rooms before they left to get married.

I returned to my room and busied myself with putting my things into the tall, mahogany dresser that stood across from the vanity, and then wandered over and seated myself in front of the mirror. I'd better comb my hair before I went down. Grandma was a stickler for neatness and she had no problem letting an offender know when he or she didn't live up to her standards. I picked up the brush and tidied my hair as well as I could. With a mop like mine, neatness was an unachievable dream. I really didn't mind Grandma's fussing though. It was as much a part of who she was as the bright, black eyes that never missed a thing. I put down the brush, and headed downstairs and into the kitchen.

Johnny and Georgie were already seated at the side of the table. Grandpa was kicked back in the chair at the head of the table, and he and Johnny were having a serious discussion about fishing. Grandpa made an effort to get Georgie involved and soon Georgie was talking animatedly in a way he never did at home.

"I reckon I'll have to take you guys fishing," Grandpa said with a twinkle in his eye. "I've been waiting for my fishing buddies. A friend of mine has a pond up north of town that feeds from a creek, so there should be some good fishing there. What do you say?"

"Oh yeah! I can't wait! Can we go

tomorrow?" Johnny enthused.

"Well, seeing as how I am off tomorrow, I do believe we can," Grandpa replied as Grandma put a large tureen of soup and a plate of cornbread on the table. "We'll leave the womenfolk to do what they want to, huh?" He looked at me and winked. "What do you have planned to do with Annie, tomorrow? I'm stealing these boys."

"Oh, I'm sure we'll find something," Grandma said airily. "William, will you say grace?"

Even here there were reminders of my stepmother. *Grace!* I thought with dismay as I bowed my head. Why couldn't she have a decent name like Linda or Sadie. Grandpa said a short prayer and then told us to dive in.

"But the soup's too shallow, Grandpa!" Johnny said pertly. Grandpa and Grandma laughed.

"That's my boy!" Grandpa said.

There was lots of talk and laughter during the meal. From time to time, I caught Grandma looking at me keenly, only to drop her eyes and compress her lips, as though there were lots of things she wanted to say. I figured she would get them said. She usually did, but for tonight, for the boys' sake, she wouldn't say them. When we were done, I offered to help her with the dishes.

"No, child, you run up and take it easy. You've had a lot on you for quite a while and you deserve a rest. I'll let you have a reprieve this one night. Grandpa is going to help the boys get ready for bed so they can get up early. You and me are going shopping tomorrow down at J.C. Penneys and C.R. Anthonys"

"Shopping?"

"Yep, Grandpa and I talked it over, and we're going to buy you some new clothes, you being in high school and all, you'll want to look your best, and then I'm going to take you to lunch down at Pop Hicks. How will that be?"

"What about the boys? Do they get new clothes too?" I could just hear Daddy's going on about playing favorites.

"Grandpa will take them tomorrow afternoon after they get back from fishing and clean up. This shopping trip is just for us girls, honey. We will pick up something special for Lanie and Janie, but I want to get you all fixed up. You're looking sort of down at heels. Can't have my girl going around looking like that."

I flushed. Grandma was saying outright what Grace had only hinted at. While I could shrug Grace off, I couldn't shrug off Grandma. She was sort of like a steam-roller. I looked at my worn skirt and shirt and winced. I hadn't really cared too much what I looked like. I had been too miserable and too busy to care. If Grandma wanted to dress me up, I decided, I would let her, and Daddy would just have to fuss. I could always point out, if he fussed, that the new clothes could count as an early birthday present. The only new thing I had had lately was the dress Grace had made me for the wedding. I *deserved* new clothes, I thought as I kissed Grandma on the cheek and hurried off upstairs. I wished I could get my hair cut, but that might have been pushing too far with Daddy. I knew Grandma would take me, if I asked, but that would have caused even more hard feelings between her and Daddy. I decided to be thankful for the clothes.

Prowling around the room, I found two of the latest fashion magazines that Grandma had bought for me and put so I could find them. I plopped myself down across the bed to enjoy them. Grandma really knew how to spoil me, I thought. I made a mental note to take the magazines home to Patty in case she hadn't gotten them yet. If she had, I'd give them to the girls to use to make paper dolls. I settled down happily to daydreams of arriving at school in triumph on Monday and making Sallie turn pea-green with envy. It was time she got her come-uppance, I thought.

After I had looked through the magazines a while and made mental notes on the things I liked, I got ready and got into bed. I snuggled down among the lavender scented bedclothes and sighed contentedly. Mama seemed so close in this house. It comforted me. I closed my eyes and slept.

CHAPTER TEN

"Well, hello, Elizabeth! How are you?" We had spent the morning shopping for new clothes and had stopped to eat. We were just finishing up our meal after a satisfying morning of shopping. Lanie and Janie had gotten new dolls, and I was now the proud owner of several stylish outfits and two new pairs of shoes. I was looking forward to wearing them come Monday.

The lady who addressed us, sat the next table, and apparently knew Grandma Jenkins well enough to be informal. "Who is that with you?"

"My granddaughter Annie. She's on a visit with me for the weekend."

"Oh my goodness! That's Annie? I would never have known her. She has grown so much. You are becoming quite a young lady, my dear." The speaker was an older woman with tight-permed, graying hair, who had stopped at our table. I stared at her angular face trying to remember who she was until a sharp look from Grandma reminded me it was rude to stare. I dropped my eyes in embarrassment.

"I don't expect you'd remember me. I haven't seen you since you were a baby," the lady went on. *That explains a lot,* I thought. "Is your Mama with you?"

I know I went white. Grandma looked sad. "Mary, I guess you hadn't heard? Ella passed away this spring."

It was Mary's turn to look shocked. "Oh no! I hadn't heard. I am so very sorry." She looked in distress from Grandma's face to mine "I didn't mean to stir up pain."

"We know you didn't. It was sudden," Grandma said, not elaborating. She folded her napkin and picked up her purse. I suspected it was to hide the sudden tears in her eyes. "If you will excuse us? We must be going," she said in a choked voice.

"Oh, Oh, of course! If you need anything, let me know," The woman moved on embarrassedly. Grandma retrieved a handkerchief from her purse and dabbed at her eyes. Her upset didn't keep her from reprimanding me when I used the napkin to wipe mine.

"Oh for goodness' sake, Annie, use this." She brought a second handkerchief out of her purse. "I'm so sorry that woman had to say anything. Here I was trying to take your mind off things and now it's all come to the forefront again." She sighed and pushed her chair back. "Try not to give people something to stare at. Tears are for at home."

I followed her to the register, where she paid for our meal, trying to do as she said. Tears were something our family didn't show much to others. We were taught to hold our heads up, no matter if our hearts were broken. Sometimes those tears spilled over the dam and out the eyes in spite of ourselves.

We were silent on the way back home. Grandma was preoccupied with her thoughts, and I didn't feel much like sharing mine. They hurt too much. I helped her carry the packages we had acquired while shopping up to my room. She excused herself for a while, saying she would just go and lie down. At loose ends, I wandered around the house, looking at the pictures of family hung on the walls. There were pictures of her and my grandpa when they were younger. They were a good-looking couple, I thought. Grandma had been beautiful, I thought loyally. She still was. There was a picture of Mama as a young girl, with my aunts. They all resembled each other strongly. I wondered what they would think of Grace, if they ever met her. I could only imagine what they thought of Daddy for marrying Grace.

On the mantel by the fireplace was a meticulously hand-tinted picture of Mama in her wedding dress in a silver-gilt frame. She looked mysterious and romantic, I thought, with her eyes lowered demurely and her hair concealed partially under a lace mantilla that spilled artfully down her back. Her perfectly manicured left hand, displaying her wedding ring, reached in an artful pose toward the profusion of flowers in her bouquet.

The hand pictured was very different from the hands I remembered. Those had been work-worn, and the fingernails, while kept neatly filed, had not achieved the perfection of this picture. The Mama I remembered had been lively and feisty and outspoken and far removed from the dreamy perfection of this portrait. Somehow her life didn't live up to the expectations that were implied in this picture of what was, to all intents and purposes, a beautiful stranger. Sighing, I moved away from the pictures and drifted into the kitchen and then out to the kitchen steps, where I plopped down and put my head down on my knees, trying to calm the wailing child within me that had awoken with my memories.

Life sure hadn't turned out well for Mama, I thought. Whatever dreams she had had when she posed for that picture were dead and buried, as she was. I wondered whether, if she had known that all her life would be was work and worry and one child after another once she married, she would have done it. *Well, that hadn't stopped Grace,* an inner voice reminded me, and I wondered again why on earth anyone would have married someone with so many children, knowing that was what she faced. Grace was just crazy, I decided. Just plain crazy. I had a crazy woman for a stepmother. I didn't want her anyway, I wanted my mother. There was no getting around that. I curled around the ache in my heart.

The warm October sun beamed down like a benediction and caressed the back of my neck. I sat there for quite a while, until the darkness inside me ebbed, and then slowly got up and made my way back into the kitchen. Grandma was up and sitting at the kitchen table with an album in front of her. When I entered, she got up and went towards the living room, carrying the album with her and beckoning me to follow.

She sat down on the couch, patting the cushion beside her. I sat down and she put her arm around me and hugged me.

"It's been really hard, Annie, for me the past few months. I can't even imagine what it's been like for you." She patted the album. "I wanted to give you this, to remember your Mama by. It's her scrap book. Whenever you feel her far away, I want you to open this and look at it. I hope it will comfort you." She handed it to me.

"I don't know if I can, Grandma. It hurts too much right now."

"That's all right. It will wait until you feel you can. You show it to your little brothers and sisters too, so they can remember their Mama that way. They are so little they won't remember much if they remember at all, but you and I—we can make sure they do."

There. She had expressed one of my fears. I was stunned to hear it spoken by someone else. I guess I had thought I was the only one who had them.

"Oh, don't look at me like that. You know it will happen if your Daddy has his way. They'll remember that woman as their mother. Janie and Lanie won't remember much at all, and the little ones won't remember. Period. I don't even know if that man will let you come again. He hates me you know."

I couldn't find words to answer that. It was

true. He made no bones about liking her. Seeing my expression, her lips thinned. She went on.

"I *told* your mother she was making a mistake in marrying him. I had high hopes she would marry a professional man, and live a better life. Who was he anyway? Some serviceman stationed at the base. She told him how I felt, and he's resented me ever since. He barely let her visit me. Now she's gone, and he's married to that woman and I can't even see my grandchildren like I want to."

I didn't know what to say to this flood of anger at things I had only guessed at. I stared at the album, uncomfortable at her critical words. For lack of any response that could make things better, I mumbled, "I'm sorry."

Suddenly aware of what she had been saying, she caught herself. "I'm sorry, too, child, and I shouldn't have burdened you with it." She patted my shoulder. "I still have you and your brothers and sisters, and I'm going to do my best to get along with your Daddy, so I can see them."

The next words that came out of my mouth startled me. "You know, Grace told him he had to let us come see you." For the life of me, I didn't know why I had recommended Grace to her.

"She did?'

"He wasn't going to let us, but she talked him into it."

"Well, good for her. Maybe I've misjudged her," I could tell Grandma was considering that possibility. "Is she good to you?"

I shrugged. Grace was as good to me as I let

her be, I thought. I wasn't going to tell Grandma that.

"Well, she better be," was all Grandma said. "Go put the scrapbook in your room and come back downstairs. You can talk to me while I make supper."

The rest of the evening passed quickly. Grandpa and the boys came in with fish stories of the one that got away and a couple of bags of new clothes. There were more dolls and stuffed animals purchased from the TG&Y downtown for the little ones. Grandpa winked when Grandma told him she had already bought the girls dolls and said that one could never have too many when one was a little girl. He insisted that I model my new clothes, so the boys had to put theirs on too. Grandma got out her old Brownie camera and took some pictures that she said she would have developed and send to me.

On Sunday afternoon we took a drive out to the new reservoir that had just been finished and drove across the top of the dam. I was white-knuckled from looking down, and I hoped Grandpa wouldn't drive off the side. The boys thought it was a great adventure though. All too soon it was time to go home. I could feel my spirits drooping as I gathered up my things, and prepared to go home. The album I left for my next visit, although Heaven knew when I would get to come again. I doubted very seriously that I could be as good as Daddy demanded. He had made the price of whatever visits I made high indeed.

Grandpa and Grandma declined to get out

when we arrived home that evening. They nodded cordially to Grace, who stood at the door watching us get out with our various bags and parcels. They did open the door to give the little girls hugs, and they promised them that they would get to come visit soon. We stood on the porch and watched them go. I think I saw Grandma dabbing at her eyes and Grandpa reaching over to pat her consolingly as we left. I hoped we would not have to wait too long for another visit.

CHAPTER ELEVEN

On Monday at school, Patty was waiting impatiently at the door for me.

"How did it go? That's a pretty outfit!"

"Do you like it? Grandma bought it for me." I twirled delightedly for her inspection. She gave me a thumbs up.

"It's a vast improvement over what you've been wearing."

"Thanks a lot,' I grumped. *Was everyone going to make remarks about how bad I had looked?*

"Oh, don't be like that. I think it's nice you got some new things. I love you no matter what you wear because you're you, but it is nice to see you looking so good. In fact, I'm jealous," Patty laughed.

"Oh phooey. What have you got to be jealous of?" Patty always had clothes that were in the latest style.

"My gorgeous friend, that's who! Wait until everyone sees you. Their eyes will pop out of their heads."

"That could be messy."

"You said it! Now come on and let's go to

class."

Sally and her crew were getting ready to sit down when we entered. Sallie looked me up and down and smirked.

"Well, look at you! Who knew you could dress like a human being."

I was speechless with rage. I wanted to scratch her eyes out for that catty remark.

Patty, seeing my anger, stepped in. "Well, dear," she said in a poisonously sweet tone, "Who knew you knew what a human being dressed like." The other girls tittered.

"You shut up, Patty!" Sallie was red with mortification.

"I'm sorry. I don't do that on command. Leave Annie alone. You've got no call to be so hateful."

"Since when do you fight her battles, Patty-cake?"

"Call me Patty-cake, again, and you will be fighting a battle with me," Patty put her hands on her hips. "Watch yourself."

The other girls tittered and Sally smirked.

"She doesn't fight my battles, Sallie Moore," I said hotly. "But I'll tell you one thing. She's a heck of a lot nicer than you are. You and your fancy clothes and hateful ways. At least she's a *true* friend. Come on, Patty." I swept past in a swish of skirts into the room, leaving Sallie and the others to stare at me unbelievingly. My going on the attack was something new to them. I vowed it wouldn't be a one-time thing. I had put up with their jibes and cattiness until now but I didn't intend to do it anymore. It was obvious that they didn't know what to make of my sudden ability to fight back.

She and her crew whispered and passed notes most of the period, to the aggravation of Mr. Johnson, who was trying to present a lesson on the Civil War. When he finally, in frustration, assigned them detention, they stared at me as though it were all my fault. I stared back defiantly. I had declared my own Civil War, and I was not about to act as though they mattered. Their harassment wouldn't be anything new to me. I hoped they would leave Patty alone though.

To my surprise they gave Patty and me a wide berth in the days to follow. There were no real confrontations. They did, however, continue to whisper and talk behind their hands. Patty treated them the same as always, politely deflecting any attempt they made to talk to her. She behaved as though they didn't matter, without seeming to be acting. It disconcerted them. *I* had to put a little more effort into ignoring them though. I didn't have her confidence, and I wasn't as comfortable in my skin as she was.

The boys' reaction to my new finery was almost as bad as I had feared.

"Whooo, what a cutie!" one boy cat-called. "I want a date!"

"Leave her alone! She's mine!" a second one, a boy I recognized from history, smirked.

"I thought she was mine!" Another snickered.

"Hey Annie! Annie! You're so pretty!"

I did my best to ignore them and sailed by

quickly. After I told Patty about it, she decided to be my escort and walk by them with me. When the remarks started, she turned and said with a pout, "Hey guys, what about me? I'm pretty too!" In response to the remarks that followed, she imitated Marilyn Monroe and blew them a scornful kiss, and then said to me, "What a bunch of jerks!"

"I'm so sick of them!"

"I imagine you are. Come on, Annie, don't let them bother you." She flounced off.

Stupid boys! I clutched my algebra book to my chest and hurried after her. Even algebra was preferable to running the gauntlet every day. I had read about running the gauntlet in a book I had checked out and I thought that pretty well described my situation. In the book though, once someone had run the gauntlet with bravery, the tribe accepted him. I didn't think that would be the case here.

Flustered, I sat down in my seat and put my books under it. One of the boys from the hall came in and sat down beside me in a seat that had been vacated by someone who had moved away. I took one side-long look at him in dismay. I was sure my torment was going to continue. My face flamed and I carefully avoided looking at him until my pencil rolled off the desk. He retrieved it for me, and I had to look at him then. I met a pair of brown eyes that weren't unfriendly.

"Thank you," I said stiffly.

"You're welcome," he replied. Just that. Nothing else. He paid no more attention to me, busying himself with taking his paper out of his book and sauntering to the pencil sharpener to sharpen his pencil. Sally and her crowd eyed him appreciatively.

Algebra was even more unnerving than usual with the boy's silent presence beside me. I pretended to pay careful attention to the problem on the board, but I absorbed nothing. The whole situation was made even worse when I was called to the board to solve one of the problems. I stood there mutely, unable to think of how to do even the first step, with the class tittering in the background.

Shut up! I thought. *Shut up! Shut up!* I let the chalk fall from my fingers and bolted into the hall, not heeding Mr. Armor's or Patty's calling my name. I didn't stop until I got to my locker. I leaned my head against the cold metal, letting the tears fall. Why didn't anyone like me? What had I ever done to anyone?

A gentle hand rested on my shoulder. I looked up, expecting to see Patty. Instead it was the boy. Shocked, I dropped my gaze again.

"Why are *you* here?"

"Why shouldn't I be?"

"Fat lot you care. Oh and don't touch me!" The hand was withdrawn.

"Well, obviously I do, since I came out here without permission."

"I guess I'm in trouble."

"We both are. Look, Annie, I'm sorry."

"For what? That I'm stupid?"

I heard him sigh, "No. I'm just sorry. I don't like how the guys treat you. I've been watching, and I don't like it. I have a little sister and I wouldn't want her to go through that."

I rounded on him. His brown eyes below the lock of dark brown hair that fell over his forehead were serious.

"Why don't you stop it then?"

"I don't really belong to that group. I kind of keep to myself on the edges and I don't think the guys would listen anyway. I just wanted you to know that not everyone is like that."

"How do you know my name?"

He smiled crookedly. "I hear it in the halls enough. My name is Luke."

I sniffed. He fished a wadded Kleenex out of his jacket pocket and offered it to me.

"It's clean. I just had it stuffed there," he said. A glimmer of a smile surfaced on his face. I smiled in spite of myself.

"Thank you. I left my purse in class." I didn't tell him I didn't have a handkerchief or Kleenex in it. Grace had insisted I carry a purse, and had stocked it with items she felt were necessary. A little package of Kleenex had been among them. I had used them all but didn't tell her I needed more. I guessed I should have, but I hated asking her for anything.

"You better go back and get it then."

"I'm not sure I can face Mr. Armor, much less anyone else right now. I feel so stupid."

"I think Mr. Armor will understand why you left. He's not a bad guy. As for my leaving, I'm not so sure, but we need to go back or we'll be in worse trouble. I couldn't just let you run out like that, so upset and all. We'd better go back though, or people will think we ran off together," a smile quirked at the corner of his mouth.

"I guess you're right." How was I going to face everyone with my face stained with tears? I had given those who didn't like me something else to taunt me with.

My dilemma was solved by the ringing of the bell.

"Come on, Annie. Let's face the music," Luke said. He didn't seem too upset at having to do that. I trailed after him, reluctantly. We waited until the classroom emptied. A few snickered as they passed me. I glared at them in return. When we went in, Patty was waiting by the desk where Mr. Armor was seated. Mr. Armor looked over his glasses at us.

"Annie, you want to tell me why you left my class?" he asked.

I shook my head, dumbly. How could I explain how I felt in a way he would understand it. It wasn't just math. It was everything. After waiting for a response, that didn't come, he shook his head and turned to Luke.

"Mr. Johnson, you want to tell me why you left?"

"I thought she might need someone to help, sir."

"Damsel in distress, huh?" He smiled wryly.

"Something like that, sir."

"Patty, I need you to go ahead and step out. You may wait outside for her. Luke, you will have three days of afterschool detention for leaving my class. I cannot allow you just to up and walk out, no matter what the reason. Do I make myself clear?"

"I understand, sir."

"Good. You may go to your next hour class."

"Thank you, sir," Luke and Patty left the room, leaving me with Mr. Armor.

"Annie, Patty has told me that you are struggling. Is that so?"

"Yes, sir."

"Why haven't you told me. You do all right on your papers."

"Patty helps me, sir."

"Ah. I see. Well, I had no idea. We must fix this problem. There remains the fact that you left my class, causing an uproar, so we must have some consequences."

"Yes, sir."

"There is also the fact that I caused you some embarrassment by calling you to the board, caused by your inability to do the problems. Do you not listen to the lesson?"

"Yes, sir, I do, but I've been distracted," To my horror, tears began to slip from the corners of my eye. Mr. Armor seemed horrified too.

"Oh good grief, don't cry. I don't know what to do with students when they cry,"

He looked so genuinely upset that I couldn't help but smile at him through my tears. He grimaced in relief.

"There, that's better. Now, I can't fix whatever is distracting you, but I can arrange for you to have a tutor so that you can understand algebra better. We can fix that. Yes, yes, that's what your consequence will be: two days a week of tutoring after school."

"But I ride a bus, sir, and my Daddy will be unhappy that I'm not home to help my stepmother with my brothers and sisters."

"I see. Well then, you will have to give up your study hall, and in the future, you will pay attention in class of course," he leaned back in the chair and steepled his fingers.

"Yes, sir."

"And Annie, I may be barging in with advice where none is wanted, but the things that we think we can't get through, we do. Focus on the task at hand. Algebra is nothing to cry over and it can be conquered if we don't let other things get in the way. Do you understand?"

I nodded my head.

"You may go."

I was happy to oblige. I gathered my books and fled. Patty met me outside. Her silent understanding made me feel better. It was good to have a friend.

CHAPTER TWELVE

Things were marginally better in the days that followed. The boys damped down their persecution for a while. The girls suspended their whispering campaign, which was a relief. Patty continued to be her cheerful self, ribbing me about Luke and declaring that she wished she had a knight in shining armor to champion her. I told her to knock it off.

Luke began to meet me each day at my locker and to walk me from class to class. It didn't seem to bother him that I didn't talk to him much. He was a constant presence at my shoulder, walking companionably by my side. I wished he would go away. I couldn't laugh and giggle with Patty as freely. For her part, she made eyes at him and tried to flirt.

He just smiled that crooked smile and kept on walking, ignoring the attempts she made to engage him in conversation. She told me she thought he was rude, but she kept on trying. His presence had the benefit of keeping the boys' torment at bay. The girls eyed him and me speculatively. I could just hear what they were thinking—probably wondering why someone like him would be interested in someone like me. He was good-looking, I had to admit, with that shock of sandy brown hair that fell over his forehead, big brown eyes, and a lean, angular face and frame. I wondered myself why he was paying so much attention to me. It couldn't be my good looks, I decided. Maybe he just felt sorry for me. I didn't like that thought at all.

Before I knew it, we were out of school for Thanksgiving, which would be a big thing this year. Daddy's relatives were to gather at our house to meet Grace and approve or disapprove of her. On Thanksgiving Day, my dad's sisters brought in pies and cakes and the latest gossip to share with her, while their husbands gathered in the living room to share the latest news with Daddy, and their children ran all around the house. Uncle George escorted Grandma Gibson in and seated her in the chair of honor, where she proceeded to hold forth on how beautiful all her grandchildren were and how she wished Gramps could have been there to enjoy them with her. She and Uncle George, for whom Georgie had been named, had travelled a couple of hundred miles to get here; a journey, she declared, that was well worth the taking.

When Grace came into the room, she held out her arms and they embraced. Grandma Gibson was very different from Grandma Jenkins. She was more laid back and less likely to fuss. On her infrequent visits when Mama was alive, she and Mama always seemed to have a special regard for each other. I had often heard them laughing over some shared joke or something one of the little ones had said or done. She was someone who was ready to love everybody—even Grace, although the marriage to her only son was as much a surprise to her as to anyone else.

Her daughters, Aunt May, Aunt Mary, Aunt Marilyn, and Aunt Martha all pitched in to help since Grace was still feeling ill and had had a woozy spell. She sat in a chair watching them, smiling wanly, and protesting that since they were her guests, she should be working instead of them—an idea they brushed aside briskly, assuring her that her condition warranted a little pampering.

What they thought of having another niece or nephew was kept to themselves. That hadn't been the case with Grandma Jenkins, who had had unkind things to say when I wrote to her to tell her. I had burned the letter so Daddy wouldn't see it. That would have caused no end of trouble that I was unwilling to have because I had a visit scheduled over Christmas break if the weather held, and I intended to get to go. My mother's sisters, in their letters back to me after I wrote them, had wished Daddy and Grace well, but they had been guarded and said little. I sensed their disapproval of the hasty marriage in their careful choice of words. I hadn't seen Mama's sisters since she died. They lived in Wynnewood and in Marlow and they didn't travel often.

Every now and then, though, they would send me a letter. Their letters were always passed along with ill will by Daddy, who seemed ready to include them in his resentment of Grandma

Jenkins. When I answered their letters, I picked my words carefully and made the letters really short and light in tone so that they wouldn't know how unhappy I was. Although they didn't say so, I was sure they knew how things stood between their mother and Daddy, and I'm sure they had a few choice things to say in their letters to her. Her daughters were very much like her—plainspoken and feisty. Maybe it was a good thing they lived so far away. There were sure to be fireworks whenever they were around. I imagined the verbal battle would have been of epic proportions.

Daddy's sisters, on the other hand, were philosophical. Things were the way they were and getting upset wouldn't change a thing. When Daddy had gotten married so suddenly after Mama died, they had kept any thoughts about that to themselves too. If anyone in town had said anything to Daddy's sisters though, I'm sure they would have changed the subject or told the offender off. They, like me, hated being the object of gossip, and they sure weren't going to give anyone any more to gossip about or allow anyone to talk badly about their only brother. Of course, no one was going to say anything to them because they lived somewhere else. They were spared that much at least. Too bad I wasn't as fortunate. I had overheard plenty, when people thought I wasn't listening.

This was my first Thanksgiving without Mama. I couldn't even think about my birthday, Christmas Day. How was I going to get through that? I was having a hard enough time with this day. I barely ate any of the turkey and dressing or pies and cakes that had been prepared. Each bite choked me. As soon as I had finished helping clean up, I excused myself and went up to my room, leaving Grace and my aunts to continue their visiting, and my cousins to help corral all the little ones.

Aunt May, of course, saw me slip out and could not leave well enough alone. Aunt May and I had always been close. She didn't have any children of her own, so I was "her" baby, she declared. She had told her sisters I was hers to spoil and brushed off any talk of favoritism with a laugh. There were plenty for the others to spoil, she said. All children should be someone's favorite.

Seeing me leave, she followed me upstairs and knocked on the door. When I told her to come in, she came and sat down beside me on the bed, where I lay face down, trying not to give in to the tears that choked me.

"Are you okay, honey?"

"Uh, huh." I turned over and sat up, face averted.

"You barely ate anything. You're missing your Mama, aren't you?" Her hand patted my shoulder. Undone by the kind tone and the gentle gesture, I began to cry. She gathered me into her arms, and I sobbed broken-heartedly into her ample shoulder. She stroked my hair.

"That's okay, honey. You just go ahead and cry. You've carried a heavy burden far too long."

"Oh Aunt May, I miss her so much," I choked

out. "When does it ever go away?"

"It takes a while, honey," She pulled back and looked into my face, her blue eyes brimming with tears of her own. "Grief is a far country that we visit for a while when our loved ones go home. Sometimes our visit is a long one, and we have a hard time finding our way back. When we do, we carry the memories, not as a burden, but as a treasure. Someday you'll be able to work through the pain and remember your Mama without tears. You will always miss her, but it will be easier." She wiped my tears with the corner of her apron. "Your Mama wouldn't want you to be always crying."

"I know," I sniffed. "It's even harder because I feel like Daddy has forgotten her."

"Now, Annie, you listen to me. Your Daddy hasn't forgotten her. He will carry her in his heart forever, just as you will. It's just that he has made a place in his heart for Grace too. She is a good woman, Annie. You need to give her a chance."

"Did she ask you to say that?"

"No, honey. It's just what I think is right. Think about what I said. You have a good heart. Listen to it"

I considered what she said, sullenly. Good woman or not, Grace's presence was a thorn in my side. Sensing that any further talk would fall on deaf ears, Aunt May left it at that and began to talk about other things, some of which made me laugh in spite of myself. She finally coaxed me downstairs to the kitchen, and got me to eat a piece of pecan pie. I discovered I was hungry and ate it with relish. I promised to ask Daddy if I could go visit her in Oklahoma City some time. She promised to take me shopping at the new mall downtown. Excited at the idea of any visit that would get me away, I told her that sounded great. Daddy, when I asked him, also thought that would be a great idea. I couldn't help contrasting his attitude at this proposed visit with his attitude toward my visiting my Grandma Jenkins. I wished things were a little bit easier there. It would have made my life simpler.

When I went back to school the Monday after Thanksgiving, the teachers announced that preparation for the Christmas program would begin in earnest. Mrs. Harriman, the drama teacher, was all a-bustle with plans. She had the artistic girls designing a backdrop and had written a play herself for the drama students to perform in addition to the songs Mrs. Colman would have us doing. We spent most of the time during her class rehearsing. Since I had a solo in the program, I was excused from having to do a part in the play, to my relief. Singing was one thing. Acting was another.

Mrs. Colman scheduled the soloists for extra practices after school, I had to approach the subject at home. I hadn't told Daddy and Grace about my solo. Now I had to tell them so I could be excused from helping Grace in the afternoon. I thought they would be unhappy about the time I would have to spend away, but they weren't.

Daddy, when I told him, smiled widely and

told me how proud he was of me. Grace told me that she thought it was lovely and mentioned that she had never heard me sing. With a start, I realized no one in that house had heard me sing since before Mama died. Mama had loved to hear me sing. A wave of sadness washed over me and I excused myself quickly. I thought I heard a little sigh as Grace and Daddy watched me leave the room. The murmur of their voices followed me as I went upstairs.

CHAPTER THIRTEEN

Mrs. Colman decided that the girls in the chorus should wear red satin dresses with sweetheart necks and full skirts and that the soloists, who would stand in the middle of the front row, would be dressed in green. The boys were to wear white shirts, green vests and black pants. I thought it sounded awful and said as much to Patty.

"I can't even think about how that is going to look," she said. "We will be really Christmassy, though."

"I'm sure Mrs. Crain will be very busy sewing vests," I said, thinking of the home-economics teacher's sour expression at the news. "She didn't look real happy."

"Oh, Mrs. Crain never looks happy about anything," Patty said airily. It was true. She didn't. I guess it was trying to teach all us girls how to cook and sew that did that to her. She wasn't really patient with me, because I had demonstrated no talent whatsoever for sewing. The machine balked every time I came near it, and I had to rip out as much as I stitched. I was glad I wasn't being asked to make anything. It would have fallen apart.

"We are going downtown to the fabric shop to get the pattern today and the satin. I'm scared," Patty went on. "My mother is *not* a seamstress and I can only imagine what the dress is going to look like. Maybe I should ask Mrs. Crain to make mine."

"If you do, you're braver than I am. Grace said she would make mine," I said. "That's one thing that she *can* do is sew."

"You are so lucky!"

"I guess," I shrugged.

"I've seen the stuff she sews for the girls. I'm surprised she doesn't sew stuff for you."

"I got new clothes. Isn't what I wear good enough?"

"Oh, Annie, knock it off. That isn't what I meant."

"Well, what did you mean?"

"I only meant that she makes a lot of stuff for the girls but I haven't heard you say she makes anything for you," Patty soothed.

"Well, I don't want her to," I grumbled. "She did offer to buy me a new twin-set and get my hair fixed at the salon once. I told her 'no.'" I didn't tell Patty how I had acted. Something told me Patty wouldn't have approved. She liked Grace, much to my disbelief and consternation. It was the one thing I couldn't agree with Patty on.

Patty was appalled. "You said 'no'? Why? If someone wanted to treat me to a new outfit and a hairdo, I'd take them up on it in a heartbeat."

"I felt like she was criticizing me. I didn't like it."

"So you did yourself out of a new outfit and a hairdo?"

"Yes I did."

"You really think she was offering just to criticize you?

"Well, look at me." I indicated my hair, which was flying wildly about my head, as usual.

Patty shook her head. "And?"

"Well, she had changed everything else around the house and put away all my mom's things and…well, I kind of felt like I was just one more thing that needed to be changed."

"Oh," Patty was looking at me with a mixture of sympathy and exasperation. "You are such a cockle burr."

"Huh?"

"All prickly and sharp. It's hard for people to get next to you. Of course," she went on, seeing my expression, "I don't have a problem since I have a thick skin…like…. like a …rhinoceros! Luke makes two of us. Good thing we have tough hides or you'd prickle us to death."

The picture of Patty and Luke as rhinoceroses made me snort with laughter in spite of myself.

"You really think I'm a cockle burr?" I asked.

"I know so," she said. "There are plenty of girls who want to be your friend but they are afraid you'll push them off."

"They do?" I was astonished. "Who would have thought?"

"Well, they do. Linda and Susie, for starters. They actually like you in spite of yourself. As for your step-mom, maybe she just wanted to be nice."

"I don't know *what* she wanted, Patty. She's all nicey-nice to the little ones, but she looks at me like I'm a snake and might bite her if I'm even half-way nice to her."

Before Patty could respond, the bell rang and she rushed off to history class, leaving me to go to home economics and face Mrs. Crain, who was still anything but happy-looking. Maybe we could be two cockle burrs together, I thought grumpily, as I mixed and measured for the biscuits we were learning to make. Because I was too busy thinking about what Patty had said, I made several mistakes, which made Mrs. Crain even grumpier.

Patty was waiting for me in front of English class as though we hadn't had the conversation. She ignored my coolness toward her, and chatted to me breezily about other things as we went in. Mrs. Oldham was lying in wait with an essay assignment. Patty rolled her eyes at me when Mrs. Oldham wasn't looking. I stuck out my tongue at her and began the assignment, hoping to get my mind off what she had said about being a cockle burr. I made good progress on several paragraphs. Patty, as usual, stared into the air or doodled. In response to Mrs. Oldham's asking her to please write, she replied innocently that she was thinking. I knew she would be pestering me for ideas after school. I didn't mind. She had practically carried me through algebra until the tutoring began. I was beginning to do better. That cheered me up. Perhaps I wasn't a total moron when it came to math.

The rest of the day passed quickly. During music class I dutifully worked hard on my solo. There were a few rough spots that Mrs. Colman drilled me on, stopping us over and over so I could finally get them. She finally pronounced my solo perfect, to the rest of the class's relief. They had been rolling their eyes and making faces by the time we finished rehearsing. Ignoring them, Mrs. Colman told me that she was pleased with my hard work. Her praise made me feel better after Patty's criticism early in the day. I wasn't used to Patty's finding fault with me. It rankled.

I returned home to find Grace trying to keep the smaller children entertained while she cooked. I scooped up the baby and herded Bobby into the living room. Johnny was lying on the floor in front of the couch, reading his homework story and Georgie was sprawled on the couch in silent communion with Miss Kitty, who was kneading her claws and purring loudly. Both boys looked up when I came into the room.

"Aw, don't bring them in here. I can't read with them in here," Johnny complained.

"Well why don't you go up to your room?"

"I like it here."

"Then you can put up with us being in here."

"No, I can't!"

The cat lowered its ears and jumped off Georgie, making a big show of being offended at all the quarreling. Georgie got up and followed her out.

"Why can't you two just stop?" he complained over his shoulder as he went out.

"It's *her* fault!" Johnny yelled after him.

I had had enough. First Patty and now Johnny. "Now listen here, you little twerp. Me and your brothers can sit in here just as well as you. It's *our* living room too!"

"Says you!"

"What on earth is going on?" Grace, looking annoyed, came to the door of the living room. "Is all the arguing necessary?"

"I just came in here to let the boys play. *He* got mad."

"Why can't she take them somewhere else? I was here first." Johnny whined.

"Why can't you go to your room to read?" I shot back.

"Oh for heaven's sake. Just stop! Johnny, go to your room. Annie, you can stay here with the boys. I need to get our meal ready, and I don't have time to referee."

"Okay, okay," Johnny said. "Do what *she* wants." He shot an angry glance at me." It won't make her like you any better."

"Johnny!" Grace said warningly, but I could see that his words had hurt.

"Well it won't. Look at her. The only thing she ever does is complain and be mean to me and she acts like she's the only one who ever misses Mama and that she needs some sort of special treatment because of it. I miss her too. I miss her too!" he sobbed and ran, stumbling, out of the living room.

Stunned, I turned to face Grace, who sank into a nearby chair and put her head in her hands. Bobby regarded her with wide eyes, a finger in his mouth. He went over and patted her comfortingly. She scooped him up, hugged him and looked up at me.

"He didn't mean that, Annie," she said.

"Yes, he did. Don't try to smooth it over, Grace. He usually tells the truth about things like that." I went to the window and gazed out. Joey toddled after me and wrapped his arms around my leg. I leaned my forehead against the cold glass of the windowpane and looked out into the yard, which was gray and desolate looking in the bleak winter light.

"You really hate me that much?" Grace asked sadly.

"Not really," I bent to pick up Joey, who was pulling at my skirt and turned back to the window. "I just wish my daddy hadn't married you so soon. You can't replace my Mama even if you do sit in her chair. Joey won't even remember her and Bobby might forget, and the twins, but I won't forget her and Georgie won't and Johnny won't. You came in when I wasn't ready and you changed everything. I can't even talk to my daddy about it because he takes your side in everything. I don't even have my Daddy anymore. If I say anything, *anything,* he says he'll send me away or he won't let me see my grandma. Do you know how that feels?" I turned back to face her, putting the baby on the floor, tears beginning to stream down my face. I wiped them with the back of my hand, impatiently.

Grace was staring at me with a stricken expression. She looked down at her hands and then back at me.

"Annie, I knew that when I married your dad, it would be hard. I told him that it was too soon. That the children might not accept me."

"But you did it anyway," I said.

"I did it anyway. I hoped that things would work out. You see, Annie, I love your dad. He is a good man. He works hard. I loved him so much I was willing to chance that. I don't want to replace your mother. She can't be replaced. I did want to, at least, be friends. I love your brothers and sisters, and I want to love you."

"But you can't."

"You push me away."

'I don't want you to love me. I want my Mama,"

"Of course you do."

I turned back to the window. With a sigh, she got up and took the little ones out of the room. I rubbed my temples to ease the throbbing that had started there and went to the bathroom and washed my face. From the kitchen I heard Joey chortling. and Bobby singing along with her as she sang a nursery rhyme. Daddy would be home soon. I hoped she wouldn't say anything or I'd be in for it. Sighing, I went upstairs to my room to do my homework. Johnny was sitting on the side of his bed looking woebegone, He looked up as I passed his room. I stood at the door and held out my arms to him. He came into my arms and embraced me tightly. I hugged him back fiercely.

"I'm sorry, Annie."

Johnny never said he was sorry. Ever. He must have felt pretty bad. I felt bad for him, and myself. To make us both feel better, I finally said, "I'm sorry too, Johnny. Tell you what. You come read in my room while I do homework. I could use some company. Where's Georgie?"

"He went out to the barn to play with the kittens. Said it was more peaceful there." Johnny plopped across my bed and opened his book. I settled down beside him with my book open.

"Does he ever say anything about, well, how things are?"

"No. Not to me. But I hear him talking to the cat every now and then."

"What does he say?"

"That he misses Mama. That he misses how things were. That he wishes everyone would quit fighting."

"Oh."

"Maybe we should quit fighting so much, Annie?"

"Yeah Johnny, maybe we should," I sighed. "Maybe we should." Trouble was, I didn't think we could or would any time soon.

CHAPTER FOURTEEN

We bought the pattern for the dress for my program. Grace said it was a simple pattern, really, and finished my dress a few days before the program. After what I'd said to her, I would have expected her to refuse outright to make it for me, but she cut out the pattern and made the dress without comment. Nor had she said anything to daddy about our conversation. I was glad she hadn't, I thought as I slipped the dress over my head. Lanie and Janie oohed and ahhed as Grace pinned the hem.

"Oh Annie, you look so pretty!" Lanie crowed.

"Yeah! Mama Grace makes such pretty clothes!" Janie said.

Mama Grace?

Grace sensed my resentment. "Their idea." She shrugged and went on pinning.

I bit back the retort I was going to make. I had meant what I said to Johnny. I was going to get along and not make waves if I had to bite my tongue into shreds. Besides, if I could hold out a little longer, I got to go to grandma's. Holding my tongue, however, was proving to be a difficult thing to do. I swallowed the angry words that wanted to be said and tried to be pleasant instead.

"Thank you for making this for me, Grace," I said tentatively.

"Thank you for allowing me to do it," she replied. "I love to sew. Now hop down off the chair and get that off so I can get the hem in it."

Patty's mom, in spite of Patty's misgivings, did a good job on her dress. I had gone over there the previous week and she had modeled it for me. Her astonishment amused me.

"Who would have thought my Mama could sew?" she said, twirling in front of the mirror and turning this way and that to admire the effect. Her dress, unlike mine was red. I was glad mine was green. The red suited her blonde coloring. It would have looked hideous on me.

"How are you going to do your hair?" She bundled her hair off her neck and eyed the effect critically.

"I don't know how I'm going to do it. At least my dress isn't red," I said, eyeing my hair equally critically in the mirror. "I don't think red is my color because it clashes so badly with my hair. It suits you though."

Remembering the visit, I once again looked into the mirror as Grace took the dress so she could hem it. *How was I going to fix this mess?* I thought despairingly, looking at the wild mop that was haloed wildly about my head. It wouldn't do anything.

Grace had paused at the door at the small sound of despair I made, and caught me trying to bundle my heavy mop of curls into something semi-acceptable. She stepped back in and said, "Could I help you with your hair? I think I can make it look nice."

"Uh, sure," I handed her the brush. I needed shorter hair. I needed smoother hair. I needed different hair entirely. If she thought she could do something with it, I was for it. After the way I had acted, I wasn't going to ask her to take me to the salon to get it fixed. I was desperate enough to take her help though. I didn't want the audience at the Christmas program to laugh at me.

She began brushing my hair with quick strokes, smoothing it as she went. "It needs to be cut and shaped."

"Daddy doesn't want it cut." There. The truth was out. One less weapon in the arsenal.

"Well, a good trimming of an inch off wouldn't hurt and I'll bet he wouldn't even notice," She laughed. I had to admit that that was probably so. "Tell you what. Let's do this." She braided my hair, pulling it sharply back from my face and caught it in a low ponytail. Deftly she arranged it into an elegant chignon and then pulled a curl here and there around my face. I stared at myself, stunned. "I don't look like me."

"And who do you look like?" she asked lightly.

In the mirror was a girl with high cheekbones and a heart-shaped face that was usually overwhelmed and lost by the curls around it. A smattering of freckles crossed the bridge of her nose, but weren't super noticeable. I stared at myself, mesmerized. I was almost—well, *pretty*. I couldn't believe it. The twins, who had wandered in and were watching in fascination, held forth once again on how pretty I looked. I thanked them solemnly and turned to Grace.

"Uh, would you do this for me the night of the program?"

"Of course," she smiled at me in the mirror. Shyly, I smiled back. Our eyes met for a moment. I thought I saw the glimmer of a tear before she turned briskly away. "Well, I need to get this hemmed before your brothers wake up from their naps." She swept the dress up and started out.

"Grace."

She stopped.

"Thank you."

"You're welcome!" She bustled out, leaving me to stare at the stranger looking back at me from the mirror.

CHAPTER FIFTEEN

The night of the program was cold and crystal clear. I dressed carefully and Grace fixed my hair. She surprised me with a gift of clip-on gold earrings and a necklace to match. Touched in spite of myself, I thanked her as she fastened the clasp. When we were done, I went downstairs to meet daddy and my brothers and sisters. For once I didn't hop and thump on the bottom of the stair. Princesses didn't do that. I concentrated on floating.

The expression on his face as he turned and saw me, startled me. It contained wonder, and pride, and dismay.

"What's wrong, Daddy."

"Nothing. My little girl has turned into a beautiful young lady."

"Aw, Daddy." I kissed him on the cheek. He helped me into my coat and turned to Grace and the kids. They were looking pretty nice too. Lanie and Janie were in blue silk dresses with puffed sleeves and skirts that belled stiffly over frothy can-cans. Johnny and Georgie were dressed up for the occasion in dark vests, pants and white shirts. Johnny's shirt-tail was coming untucked. I grabbed him and tucked it in.

"Let's go. I want to get good seats!" Daddy said, opening the door.

A chorus of me-too's followed. Daddy and I helped Grace get the little ones' coats on. "I have a surprise for you all," Daddy laughed as we went out the door. "Your pumpkin awaits!" He said to me with a little bow.

Instead of the old pickup, a shiny, blue station wagon stood in the yard. Over the hubbub of excited exclamations, he met Grace's eyes. "Been saving up overtime for years to get this."

The little ones shrieked their approval and climbed in. Georgie and Johnny claimed the space in the back, and Daddy ceremoniously ushered first me, then Grace, into the front seat. We were going to the concert in style.

Patty was waiting for me backstage in the auditorium. Her eyes widened when she saw me. Her astonishment was shared by several of the popular girls, who stared and whispered. A boy stationed on the risers wolf-whistled, causing everyone to turn around and look. I blushed and turned away from them to Patty.

"Wow. Where is Annie and what did you do with her? You look wonderful!"

"Thank you! You look pretty good yourself." She did. Her blonde curls had been swept into a French twist. Pearls gleamed at her neck and on her ears.

Mrs. Harriman bustled by in search of her actors and actresses. She made a big business of getting them together and in their places. The play was to be presented first, so I had even more time to be nervous. Mrs. Colman found us and herded us into line just before it ended. By now my mouth was dry with the fright of singing in front of all those people. A chorus of murmuring voices, punctuated by the occasional cry of a young child was building slowly in the auditorium. At her signal we filed on stage and took our places. In spite of her students' misgivings, somehow Mrs. Coleman's plan for the chorus's dresses worked. Mrs. Crain actually beamed at the fruit of her efforts from the front row, which had been reserved for the teachers.

Most of the musical program was a blur to me, except for the song in which I was to sing the solo. The soft strains of Silent Night and the special descants written for it wafted over the audience. When the time came for my solo, I stepped forward into the spotlight and took a deep breath, wishing Mama were there to hear me and hoping that somehow, there up in heaven, she *could* hear me. My nervousness evaporated. I would sing for her. I lifted my voice, singing with all my heart, becoming once again part of the music. When the last strains of my solo died away, the audience sat perfectly quiet and still for a moment and then broke into thunderous applause. The program was over.

Daddy and Grace and the little ones met me outside after the performance. Grace had tears in her eyes and Dad looked proud.

"That was so beautiful, Annie," Grace said.

"Yes, it was." Patty's father had come up behind me. I jumped. Patty and her mother stood beaming beside him. I smiled back.

"Thank you!"

"Best song in the concert," said Patty's mom.

"That's my Annie!" Johnny said.

I felt shy and uncomfortable with all the praise, but it was nice. I thanked each one who came up to me and praised my performance.

The next day Mrs. Colman told me how pleased she was with my singing and that I should consider a career in music. I told her I would definitely think about it. I can't say I was too worried about something that appeared to be so far into my future. I was more concerned with getting through my first birthday and Christmas without my Mama's being there. I didn't know how on earth I was going to do that, never mind think about a career in music. Just getting through the immediate future was hard enough.

Grace and Daddy had gone to town while we were in school, and they had brought home a pine tree to put up. They and the little ones had decorated it with the glass baubles and garland and lights from our previous Christmases. I took one look at the tree and fled to my room away from the memories it called up. I couldn't bear it. Before long I heard Daddy's footsteps on the stairs. He knocked at the door.

"Annie? Can I come in?"

I rolled over and sat up. "Yeah."

"Grace says I should come talk to you," he sat down heavily beside me. "She says it bothers you that we don't talk."

"Uh huh," I said around the lump that was gathering in my throat. "How does she know?"

"She's a very perceptive woman and she sees more than you think. Uh…look…uh…I know this is really hard for you. It's uh…hard for...uh...me too."

I looked at him, unconvinced. It didn't use to be hard to talk to me. Of course, that was before Mama died and we got crosswise over Grace. Perceptive or not, she was still a thorn in my side. I didn't know if I liked her telling Daddy to talk to me.

"I uh …put up the tree for the little kids' sake. Grace said we could do without it if we needed to, but I thought we should for them."

"Oh."

"I'm glad you and her are getting along better," he put his arm around my shoulders. I leaned my head against his shoulder.

"Yeah. I am trying…mostly for Georgie's sake. He hates it when any of us fight."

"That's a good reason."

"It's as good a one as I've got right now, Daddy."

"It's a start."

"Daddy, I've had a really hard time with all this." I turned to face him.

"I know. Grace told me."

"Daddy, can I tell you how I feel and you won't get mad at me?"

"I will try not to."

"Daddy, when you married Grace, I felt you

just threw Mama away. I felt like you just threw me away and you wouldn't listen. And then she came in and changed everything, and I felt I lost what little bit of Mama I had. I know she tries, and I'm going to try, but it is so hard. I'm trying to understand, but I'm not there yet. I know I've acted awful. Everyone has told me in different ways."

He sighed, looked down at his hands, and looked up again. "I'm sorry, Annie. I shouldn't have sprung it on you that way and just demanded that you accept it. I should have known better. I loved your Mama, Annie. No one will ever take her place in my heart. But I looked at you trying to take her place and do all the things she used to do, and you were just a kid, and I felt awful. I met Grace while I was working on a job. I didn't mean to fall in love so quickly, but I did, and she did. She was even willing to take on you kids. Not every woman will step in and love another woman's kids. I needed her, Annie, and she needed someone to love. I felt it was the right thing to do. There isn't a day goes by that I don't miss your Mamma, and Grace knows that and loves me anyway. It takes a big-hearted woman to understand that, and know that it isn't about her. Grace is one of those women. I will never do anything to hurt her or let anything come between us."

"Not even me."

"Not even you. I love you. You are my child. But I need you to show respect. I am not asking you to love her. I can't force you to do that. I know things have been tough on you. I'll try and do the best I can to help you and your brothers and sisters get through this. It's tough on all of us."

I walked over to the window. I heard him get up and walk towards the door, "Daddy?"

"Yes?"

"I love you."

"I love you too, Pumpkin." He shut the door carefully behind him.

CHAPTER SIXTEEN

Somehow I made it through Christmas day—my first Christmas without Mama, my first birthday without Mama. That was really hard. I watched the kids opening their presents under the tree and remembered how things had been last Christmas when Mama was still with us.

I wasn't too interested in opening presents, even though the biggest package was for me and turned out to be a beautiful turquoise twin set. I managed to smile weakly and thank Grace, who was watching me anxiously as I opened it. I suddenly teared up. I had been doing that a lot lately. I excused myself and dashed for the bathroom, where I splashed water on my face.

"She didn't like it, did she?" I heard Grace ask.

"Either she really didn't, or she really did," Daddy rumbled from his seat in the big chair where he had been playing Santa Claus, complete with a red Santa hat.

I supposed that I'd better come out of the bathroom. I didn't want them to know that my tears had nothing to do with the present they'd given me. I patted my face dry and gazed into the mirror at my red-rimmed eyes and sighed. Green eyes and red eyeballs…at least I was in the spirit of the season, I thought as I headed back to the living room, which was full of noise and excited little shrieks as the other kids discovered the contents of the presents addressed to them. Grace, who had been laughing at the baby, who had climbed into a box and was covered up in wrapping paper and playing peek-a-boo, looked up inquiringly as I entered.

"Thank you, Grace. It's really pretty," I said as sincerely as I could.

"I'm glad you like it," was all she said, but her face lost some of the wary look she often had when dealing with me. "Why don't you go try it on? I'd like to see what it looks like on you."

"Sure," I was grateful for the chance to exit. I scooped up the box and headed upstairs. Once I reached the sanctuary of my room, I sat down on the side of the bed, box in hand and let myself really cry. Maybe if I could get all cried out, I wouldn't suddenly be suddenly spouting tears like a waterfall at the most inconvenient moments— like the middle of math class, or while eating my lunch. If Patty were with me, she would reach over and pat me on the back, which generally made me feel better. The other kids tended to eye me as though I had suddenly sprouted horns. All that crying made them uncomfortable. They had quit harassing me, but I was still an oddity. Luke didn't seem bothered though. I would have thought all that crying would have run him off. It didn't. He would just sit silently beside me, lending me the comfort of his presence. I had gotten used to his being there, but I wasn't sure I'd ever be comfortable crying in front of him when I couldn't even be comfortable crying by myself. After a few moments, I made myself stop sobbing and reached for a handkerchief and blew my nose. "Oh great," I thought. "I'll look like Rudolph now." I took the turquoise twin set out of the box and stroked its softness. It was nice of her to get the twin set for me after all the times I had been rotten to her. I slipped my old red sweater over my head, put on the twin set, and assessed myself in the mirror. "Yep, Rudolph all right. Matches the green eyes and red eyeballs. Merry Christmas to me!" I picked up the brush and twisted it up in the way Grace had taught me to do. Wow, I looked grown up. Suddenly wanting everyone to see how I looked, I clattered down the stairs, giving the last step an extra thump.

Daddy and Grace looked up at that thump. Daddy smiled widely.

"Who have we here? Did Annie bail out the window and let in a blue bird? You look really pretty, honey. Grace, she's growing up on us!"

"Yes, she is," Grace agreed. Her eyes met mine and I smiled, this time a genuine smile. For a moment, I forgot we weren't friends.

CHAPTER SEVENTEEN

The weather held enough over Christmas break for a visit to Grandma Jenkins. This time Lanie and Janie got to go. I spent a lot of time in my upstairs room during this visit, mostly to get away from their noise. They demanded Grandma's full attention, so I was left more or less to entertain myself. I took Mama's old scrap book album from the bottom drawer where I had stowed it. I hadn't looked at it at all after Grandma first gave it to me, but I thought that maybe, it was time. Here in Mama's old house, amid the comfort of the things in her room, I might be brave enough to endure it. On this particular evening, I wandered down the hall and opened the door.

The room was as I remembered it. Grandma Jenkins hadn't changed anything. Mama had loved lavender and her room reflected this, from the pale lavender curtains at the windows to the trim on the small lamp on the bedside table. There hadn't been a twin bed for Mama when she was a girl. She had had a full bed and it dominated the room, which was large and sunny on this late December day. I remembered cuddling with her in that bed. I crawled onto the bed, and settled myself with the scrapbook on my knees.

Mama had started keeping the scrapbook when she was ten. Tucked among the browning pages were party favors and old pictures of her as a little girl, knobby-kneed in her Brownie uniform and beanie, pictures of her on a horse that was twice as tall as she was. I hadn't known Mama knew how to ride. It was a revelation to me. On another page was a scrap of newsprint, yellowed and brittle now, that announced her attendance at a birthday party. A yellowed picture on still another page, showed her and other girls in home economics class. She was holding a pie and grinning at the camera as if to say, "See what I made?" I chuckled, wondering what it tasted like. Mama's pies had been legendary for their heavy, doughy crusts. I wondered if she had made a good grade on that pie. I remembered with a smile that she was much better at making cakes than pies.

Going through the scrapbook, I saw the progression of years. I read the snippets of poetry she had stashed among the pages, savoring these glimpses into the young girl that Mama had been. There were letters from pen pals and dried, pressed flowers she had saved from special events. Those must have had special meanings attached, although she hadn't seen fit to label them. I wished she were there to tell me about them. Sighing, I closed the book and wandered downstairs.

Grandma was helping the twins cut out paper snowflakes, which they proudly showed me when I came into the kitchen. Grandpa was in his favorite chair in the living room, dozing—or pretending to. He opened one eye when I came in and then winked it.

"Grandma tell us a story!" Janie demanded. "Tell us about the olden days."

Grandma laughed. "The olden days, huh?"

"Yeah! You're real old," Lanie said, not to be outdone. "So tell us about when you were little."

"Lanie Gibson, don't you be rude!" I exclaimed.

I heard a snort of suppressed laughter from Grandpa. Grandma shot him an exasperated look, and then turned back to the two little girls, who were waiting for a story with wide-eyed innocence.

"Say you're sorry!" I demanded.

"It's all right," Grandma said. "They're just little, and have to learn manners yet. Girls, it is bad manners to refer to a grown woman's age."

"Why?" Janie asked.

"Because that's the way it is. Ladies don't refer to their ages."

"Well I'm six, and I don't mind at all," Lanie declared.

"You will when you are older," Grandma said firmly. "Now, what kind of story do you want to hear?"

"Tell us a story about Mama," I said, before either of the twins could open their mouths. "Tell us about when she was a little girl." I quelled the girls' objections with a glare. I was determined they would hear something about Mama. They were in a fair way to forgetting her. Grandma, after looking at my determined face, settled back in her chair. I retrieved a pair of scissors from Lanie just as she was about to snip a piece of

Janie's hair.

"You know better than that!"

"I wasn't going to cut it!"

"You were too. Don't lie." I took the other pair of scissors from Janie, who was now eyeing Lanie with a calculating look on her face.

"I'm not lying!" Janie pouted.

"Oh, for Pete's sake! I saw you. Daddy would be so mad if you did that. And he'd be mad at me and Grandma for letting you. Why can't you behave?"

"I am being have,"

"Girls, girls, let's not bicker," Grandma broke in. Then she laughed. "Seeing all this puts me in mind of when your Mama did this to one of her sisters."

"She did?" Lanie asked.

"Yes, she did. She gave Sheila a haircut, and oh what a haircut that was! I had to trim the rest of it and Sheila went around looking like a boy for a while. She never quite forgave your Mama for that one. Your grandpa made it worse by calling her 'Spike.'"

Grandpa by now was openly chortling.

"It wasn't funny, George."

"Well, I just figured I'd got my boy. Tried to teach her to fish too. She didn't like it any more than Annie does though," He chuckled reminiscently.

"Grandpa, will you take us fishing?" Janie asked.

"Depends," Grandpa said mock seriously. "You know you'll have to cut your hair and handle worms and all that don't you?"

"Ew! Worms?" her look of horror tickled him even more.

"Well, I guess we could forgo the haircut, but you have to be able to bait a hook, and sit real still and be quiet."

"I can bait a hook, Grandpa!" Lanie said. "I like worms."

It was all I could do not to shake my head. The last time she had had contact with a worm was when Johnny was chasing her with it. She had run around the room screeching with Johnny in hot pursuit. The chase had ended when I had put out my foot and tripped Johnny. The worm went flying—right into her hair. Hysterics followed, both Johnny's at being tripped, and hers at having a worm in her hair. I had gotten in trouble, but it was worth it. He hadn't chased her with a worm since.

Grandpa was mightily entertained at her assertion.

"It just so happens I have some worms out there in my bait bucket. Let's go get acquainted."

"You do?" Lanie said, her eyes widening.

"I do. Come on, let's go see how many I have," he started up out of his chair. It was all I could do not to snicker. Served her right for lying. He headed for the door.

"George Monroe Jenkins, don't you bring that nasty bait bucket in here!" Grandma fussed.

"I won't make a mess. It's only a little dirt and worms after all," the kitchen door snicked shut behind him. Grandma sighed, and Lanie looked apprehensive.

"Maybe one will crawl up your arm and into your hair," I said. Her eyes widened. Grandma huffed her disapproval at my teasing.

Grandpa stepped back in with the white bait bucket, set it down, and beckoned her over. He dug a minute in the black soil and came up with a large, wiggling, gray worm.

"Here you go!" he said, offering her the worm. She shrank back. "It won't bite. It's a friendly little guy. Put your hand out."

She put her hands behind her back.

"I thought you said you liked worms," he said.

"I do. I just don't want to touch them."

"Hmmm. I see. Well, you can't go fishing with me until you can touch them." From the look on her face, I figured it would be a long while before she did.

He transferred the worm back into the can, hiding his smile as she exhaled in relief and taking the bait can outside. I rounded on her.

"Lanie, you just told two stories in the last ten minutes. You need to quit. You knew you were going to cut Janie's hair, and you darn sure don't like worms. What on earth has gotten into you? Grandma and Grandpa won't know when you're telling the truth if you keep that up."

Her lower lip trembled and a tear slipped from the corner of her eye. I wished I thought that she was really sorry, but I knew she was an accomplished little actress.

"Annie, now. Leave her be. She's sorry, aren't

you, honey?" Grandma soothed, reaching to draw her to her. She nodded and threw her arms around Grandma's neck and sobbed piteously.

Oh great. Now she'll be worse, I thought.

"Grandma, she does this all the time. She plays Grace like a cheap fiddle. All she has to do is boohoo and she's off the hook." At this Lanie began to sob even more loudly.

"I want my Mama Grace!" She wailed. At this, Grandma disentangled herself from Lanie and held her at arm's length.

"Grace is not your Mama. Your real Mama is looking down from heaven and crying right now. Stop that crying. Stop it now." Her sharp tone caused the wailing to stop abruptly. Lanie looked at her, lip out, snuffling. "Do you know I am your real Mama's Mama? It hurts my feelings for you to cry for someone else." To my horror, Grandma began to cry. Lanie looked stricken.

Little brat. I thought. Then, *There's no telling what she will go home and tell Daddy and Grace—or Janie either, for that matter.* Janie was regarding the whole scene with a troubled expression. Her fingers, which she tended to chew on when she was anxious, were creeping towards her mouth. About that time Grandpa came in, and looked astonished.

"All this blubbering over a worm?" he asked. I shook my head at him and he raised his eyebrows and retreated back to his chair. I heard the rattle of a newspaper. I'm sure he wasn't reading, but was listening closely. I hoped I could fix the situation a little bit.

"Janie, Lanie, you come upstairs with me a while. Come on, now. I mean it. Get a move on!" I took each girl by the arm and propelled them towards the stairs. Lanie looked backwards at Grandma, who had cradled her head on her arms, and dragged her feet. I practically pushed both girls up the stairs. When we were in my room, I shut the door and leaned against it. The girls sat on my bed, and watched me warily. They were sure I was going to lose my temper. I really wanted to, but I took a deep breath. My silence unnerved them more than a tirade. Lanie began to fidget uncomfortably. I let her, thinking of what I could say that would smooth things over in their minds. If they went home and told Daddy and Grace tails, we wouldn't get to come back.

"Lanie," I finally said. "Are you sad about Mama?"

She nodded solemnly. Janie nodded too.

"Well, Grandma is real sad too because Mama was her little girl, and she misses her very, very much. She is afraid you'll forget Mama," *She wasn't the only one*, I thought as I said this.

"She is?" Lanie's blue eyes were wide.

"Yes, she is, so we have to watch what we say, so we won't hurt her feelings. You can call Grace 'Mama Grace' at home." I winced inwardly as I said that, feeling disloyal to Mama's memory. "That way, we won't hurt Grandma's feelings."

"I didn't want to hurt Grandma's feelings," Lanie's eyes welled up with tears. This time I thought they were sincere.

"Well, you did. First you told lies and then

you hurt Grandma's feelings. You mustn't tell lies, and you don't need to be fake crying just to get sympathy when you get in trouble. Do you understand me? Janie, you are not in trouble, so quit chewing your fingernails. We are going to go down there and you, Lanie, are going to tell her you're sorry and you are going to mean it," I said fiercely. She nodded. "Come on, now. Let's go down there and get it done." I herded the girls to the door.

Grandma had recovered somewhat by the time we went down. Lanie hovered at the door of the kitchen, uncertain, until Grandma opened her arms. Lanie fled into them and was enveloped in a tight hug that muffled her apology.

"I'm sorry too, baby, I love you very, very much." Grandma kissed the top of her head and reached an arm out for Janie, who wrapped her arms about Grandma's neck and kissed her noisily. I breathed a sigh of half-relief. For now, peace was restored. Lord help us all if they went home and told about this. I guess I would have to deal with it when and if it happened.

It occurred to me that our being there was both a comfort and a painful reminder of Mama's loss for my Grandma. The unaccustomed thought sent me to join the little girls in giving Grandma hugs and kisses. In the living room, I heard Grandpa clear his throat as though there were a frog in it, and the rattle of the newspaper. I left Grandma then, and went and hugged my Grandpa, who was not as open as my grandma, in his grief.

CHAPTER EIGHTEEN

On the first day back to school, Patty shrieked excitedly when she saw my twin set. She wanted one just like it, she declared, only in pink. She came up with an idea that she and a couple of other girls we had been having lunch with should all buy one in different colors. I wasn't too crazy about the idea, and neither were the other two girls. After a few skirmishes, Patty figured out that she wasn't going to get her way and left it alone. I was relieved. I'm sure the other girls were too.

I don't know how I would have gotten through the winter without her. It was so gray and depressing. In January we had ice storms, and the resulting ice hung on for weeks. My family had been cooped up with each other in the house and were really getting on each other's nerves. The girls nearly drove us all wild with their complaining, and Johnny and Georgie almost came to blows on a couple of occasions. There was no place in the house that wasn't full of children and no place to be peaceful. All that didn't help my mood any. I would come to school with a sad face and a bad attitude. She would take one look at my face and find a way to make me laugh.

Luke had resumed shadowing me, as though we hadn't been apart. I thought he would have gotten tired of being ignored, long ago, but he was still hanging around. Patty teased me unmercifully about him. I told her to shut up, but I wondered why he was still hanging around me.

School stretched out in a bleak prospect of seemingly endless succession of days until Easter. I hated this part of the year. Although there weren't any breaks, at least the school days were a change from the tedium of home and constant chores. I couldn't even flee to the creek right now for privacy. It was iced over, and Daddy forbade me to go near it during the winter. He had no wish for me to fall through the ice and drown, he said. It was bad enough that I couldn't stay away from there in the summer.

He did, however, allow me to go to Patty's once a week. I think he did it for Grace's sake. When I wasn't there, she didn't have to deal with me. I tried hard to be civil, but sometimes I slipped and answered in a sharp tone that drew a pained look from her. I would have liked to tell her off, but I couldn't. Daddy's threats hung over my head.

The little girls, to my relief, hadn't said anything to them on our return from our last visit with Grandma and Grandpa Jenkins. I didn't say anything about it either. I didn't want to remind them because there was no telling how the story would come out of their mouths, and Daddy wasn't inclined to hear any kind of defense for his former mother-in-law. It wouldn't take much for him to forbid our visits.

I loved visiting Patty's house. Her mother was a large, easy-going woman with a carefree laugh. She thought I was funny, even when I wasn't trying to be, but I never felt she was being mean. Her good humor was infectious. She treated me like a long-lost daughter who had come home. Patty and I were allowed to help ourselves to the brownies that seemed to always be baked, and once, she even joined us in trying to twist—an effort that made Patty and I cry with laughter. It felt good to laugh. I didn't get to do much of that at home. It seemed as though all I did at home was referee little kid fights. Grace's nerves, frayed with pregnancy, caused her to withdraw to the sanctuary of hers and daddy's room, leaving me to deal with it all. It was a relief to come to Patty's and unwind. How Grace coped on those days, I didn't know, and I didn't care. At least I was free for that afternoon.

I didn't dare complain to Daddy about the state of affairs at home. He was working long hours and was exhausted when he came in. He made it clear he didn't want to hear any complaining. At least it was fairly quiet after he got home, for that very reason. Offenders were sent to bed quickly. It didn't take Johnny and the twins long to learn that. I was grateful for a little peace to get my homework done. The teachers had decided, apparently, that we didn't have enough to do. I did my homework at odd moments wherever I could find a peaceful place. I was barely maintaining C's.

On this particular afternoon, I was lolling on the couch at Patty's. We were listening to Neil Sedaka singing about how breaking up was hard to do. Patty was singing along at the top of her voice, slightly off-key, and pretending to be giving a performance. She had me giggling with her eye rolls and exaggerated dance moves.

When the song came to an end, she took the record off the player and collapsed on the couch.

"Wow, Patty, you could make millions with that act," I said.

"Yeah, I can see my name in lights now. Look out, world!" She batted her eyelashes and looked coyly at me.

"I'll be your manager."

"No way! You should be the singer and I'll be *your* manager. You sing way better than I do."

"Maybe, but I don't have your star quality."

"Well, maybe we can be a double act. Come on, let's go do a song for Dad.

Her dad was in their den, watching *Dragnet*. He shushed us until the program was over, and then asked what we wanted. Patty grabbed him by the hand and dragged him out of the den and guided him onto the couch, where he blinked good-naturedly at us and folded his arms.

"Well, I'm waiting."

We put the record on and launched into our best imitation of the Beatles. He started laughing, and all of a sudden, he joined us, taking Patty's hand and lip-synching to "I Wanna Hold Your Hand." He was so funny, that I had to drop out from laughing at him. I wished my dad could be this much fun. Patty was in fits of giggles. Her mother came from the kitchen to see what was happening and then danced back out. I couldn't, in a million years, imagine my Daddy or Grace doing such things. Life was too serious. Mama might have, had she lived, but she wasn't here anymore. Abruptly, my pleasure vanished. I quit laughing and sat down.

"You okay?" Patty stopped clowning and bent over me concernedly.

"Yes," I lied, hoping that God wouldn't get me for lying. "Just out of breath from laughing at you two," I continued lightly. Her face told me that she knew it was an excuse. Her dad patted me on the shoulder and wandered back to his den.

"Well, guess we better settle down and do our homework then," Patty said after a moment. "Mrs. Oldham is going to kill me with all those essays."

"We only have one a week."

"That's one too many."

"Did you get the history assignment done?" I was grateful for the change of subject.

"No. More writing. I hate it,' she rolled her eyes. "He and Mrs. Oldham must connive to make me miserable."

"Oh come on now," I said. Secretly I agreed with her though. Everyone had the conviction that the teachers conspired to make our lives miserable. "Guess we'd better get started." I would have to help her get her thoughts organized. She always got her papers back filled with red marks. It was a wonder the paper didn't bleed. She tended to write as she thought—in short bursts with periods after each burst. I'd read some of the notes Mrs. Oldham had put on her papers, and I felt sorry for her. I didn't know why someone who could do a complex problem in algebra couldn't string her words together so that they made sense, but Patty couldn't.

We trailed up to her room and settled down on the floor to work. I had to be home in a couple of hours. Patty's parents had invited me to stay for dinner. *Dinner* they called it. We called it *supper*. Another difference. I let my gaze wander around Patty's room. Patty was really fond of ruffles and the color blue, and this was reflected in the baby-blue, ruffled bedspread and ruffled curtains. A window seat with a thick blue cushion and plump throw pillows dominated one wall. I imagined being able to curl up there and read. Her room seemed like a small piece of heaven to me, right down to the cushy carpet we were sprawling on now, and she had it all to herself. No squalling, bawling, annoying little sisters to have to share it with. I sighed and turned my attention to the biology lesson. Labeling frog parts. Johnny would love that one.

CHAPTER NINETEEN

School was abuzz. Valentine's Day was drawing near and the love bug had bitten. That meant valentines stuffed in lockers, and sometimes a bouquet of flowers presented to some girl who was worthy of a favor. Sallie and her crowd had paired off with the athletes. Sallie was hanging out with a hefty quarterback from the football team. It didn't matter to her that he wasn't too good looking. All that mattered was the prestige of being the star quarterback's girl. They were a strange-looking pair. She was so short and he was so tall. When she took his arm, she had to reach up to hold it. It struck me as slightly ridiculous. I said so to Patty, who agreed wholeheartedly.

Even Patty seemed to have been bitten. She had a crush on a tall, blonde basketball player and worshiped him from afar. Every conversation managed to be about the virtues of her dream boat. Although I didn't say anything, I was impatient with all the mooning around. I wasn't interested in whether he had noticed her or not. I knew he hadn't, or she would have swooned away on the spot. She didn't appreciate my pointing that out to her. When we walked downtown to the drug store after school, bundled up against the cold, she always insisted on taking the several blocks' detour to walk by his house. I don't know what she would have done if he had come out and confronted her. I figured I would have had to tote her home or catch her as she ran.

Luke, as always, was my patient shadow. When Patty twitted me about his being in love with me, I always shushed her. I told her I wasn't interested in having a boyfriend right now. Besides, Daddy would have a conniption if he thought a boy was hanging around me. He told me I couldn't have a boyfriend until I was sixteen, and then he would think about it. I wondered what Daddy would think of Luke if they ever met. I wondered if Daddy would scare Luke off. He wasn't my boyfriend, exactly, but I'd grown used to his presence. When he was by my side, the boys didn't give me grief. Sallie had tried to dig out whether or not we were an item, but hadn't had much luck. I wasn't talking, and neither was he. Her efforts to flirt (this was before the football player) had been met with a blank stare. Miffed at this rejection, she let people know that she thought he was odd. He didn't seem to mind.

When I asked him why he hung around with me, he just smiled and said, "I thought you could use a friend." Patty's questions were politely deflected, so I really didn't learn anything that way. We spent our time making up wild stories about his being a secret agent in the witness protection program, or a boy with a tragic past he was trying to forget. Our curiosity had grown daily.

One day, when he met me at my locker as usual, I rounded on him. "You know, you've followed me around most of the year and I don't even know anything about you except your name."

"What do you want to know?" He smiled his crooked smile. Some girls might have found it attractive, but after a whole semester of his following me around, I found it merely annoying. He was like an older brother who wouldn't leave me alone by this time.

"Well, when Patty asks, you won't answer," I told him.

"Well, I was waiting for *you* to ask."

I stared at him incredulously. *Waiting for me to ask?* "You have got to be kidding me."

"No, I'm not. I don't know if you've noticed, but you let Patty do all the talking. I want to talk to you, not her."

That statement made me distinctly uncomfortable. I took my books out of the locker, slammed the door, ducked my head and took off down the hall. He followed me.

"There you go! Every time I try to talk to you, you clam up and won't say anything and you take off. Stop just a minute!"

I stopped and turned to face him. What on earth was I supposed to say that he could possibly be interested in? I could feel my face freezing up as I told him as much.

"Well, for one thing, you could tell me about yourself. All I really know is you're in my math class, the guys pick on you, and you hang out with

Patty all the time."

"I don't need a protector!"

"I didn't say I wanted to be one."

"Then why do you hang around me all the time? It's not as if we were a couple or anything," I said.

"Why not? Maybe I'm just interested in you. I do want to be friends."

I started walking again, quickly, digesting this statement. That was the last thing I needed—a boy interested in me. Daddy would flip. He strode beside me, easily keeping up, taking one stride to my two steps. I had a hard enough time at home without getting grief over that. I stopped and looked into his face, which was serious and not at all mocking.

"Friends is all I can be right now, and I'm not sure how much I can be of that," I said.

"Well, it's a start. Let's see, I'm not sure we've properly introduced ourselves to one another. We sort of picked up in the middle. Luke Edward Adams at your service, ma'am," he sketched an elaborate bow, causing a group of girls passing by to giggle wildly.

"Oh for Pete's sake! Stop that!" I hissed.

"All right, but I think you owe me your full name in return," he said, grinning. "Turnabout's fair play, you know."

"Anne Marie Gibson,"

"Got your name, now I need your rank and serial number."

"I'm not in the service, you dope!"

"Well, listen to that! The friendship is

progressing. She's calling me names already," he said to the air, and then to me. "Seriously, I want to know more about you, and I want to talk to you without Patty's being around because I can't get a word in edgewise. Here she comes now." He strolled off, leaving me to stare after him.

Patty's sharp eyes missed nothing.

"What on earth was he saying to you?" she asked. I blushed.

"Hmm? Oh, nothing," I said. *And everything.*

"Well it must have been something! Well come on, we'll be late to class. Mrs. Oldham will have our hides."

I followed her down the hall, and had to apologize to one of the seniors when I bumped into her and made her drop her books.

"It's okay," the senior smiled as I helped her gather them up.

"Gee, Annie, watch where you're going," Patty admonished. "Get your mind on business."

I had my mind on business. My business. It was all I could think of.

CHAPTER TWENTY

Patty was coming over today to spend the afternoon. I stared out the window as I waited for her to come. It was raining, a soft, gray drizzle, just like it had been on the day of Mama's funeral, which I found depressing. When she got there I greeted her with relief. She had brought a new teen magazine for me to look at and we headed up the stairs. She made herself at home and sprawled across the bed, idly flipping pages in it, while I sat in front of the mirror and tried to comb my curls into submission. I finally flung the comb down in disgust.

"I give up. I don't care what I do, I look like a dust mop."

"You do not," Patty said. She scrunched up her face as she considered me. "You are, actually, kind of pretty."

"Me?" I snorted, turning back to the mirror. "You're just saying that to be nice."

"No really. You have really spectacular coloring. I would kill for that shade of red," she said. "You just don't have a really good picture of yourself. *Luke* seems to like you."

"Right," I mumbled as I retrieved the brush

from under the bed. He was, indeed, showing signs of wanting to be more than a friend. Trust her to mention that. I still didn't know what to do about it. It gave me butterflies. Patty, oblivious to the discomfort she had evoked, went back to flipping pages in the magazine. After a while she looked up.

"When is the new baby due?"

"Huh?" I was still thinking about Luke and my predicament. "Oh, in July, I think."

"Are you excited?"

"Not really," I said with all the nonchalance I could muster. A vision of my mother in the coffin with the baby tucked in came into my mind and made me catch my breath as the tears threatened to spill again. That baby would have been almost a year old now, if she had lived. "I mean, I have how many brothers and sisters?" I joked to cover up my thoughts. There was no use depressing Patty, who was looking at me with a mixture of surprise and alarm. I turned back to the mirror and made a big business of gathering my hair into a high ponytail. It looked more like a squirrel tail, I thought disgustedly, and huffed a sigh.

"Well, if you don't want it, send it to me. I'll spoil it," Patty said finally. "I'm going to come over every day to see it. The baby will call me Aunt Patty," she pronounced solemnly.

"I declare, Patty, sometimes you are just plain goofy," I picked up a pillow from the bed and whacked her with it.

"What's goofy about that?" She hurled the other pillow at my head, narrowly missing me, and then dived off the bed head first to retrieve it. She climbed back on the bed and balled it up and rested her chin and hands on it.

"Oh, nothing I guess." I decided to change the subject. I picked up the magazine, which had fallen to the floor during our tussle and opened it. "Hey, did you see the dress that model has on. I wish I had the nerve to cut my hair that short. Shoot, I wish I had the nerve to wear my dresses that short."

"Don't change the subject," Peggy said amiably, but settled down to look at the rest of the magazine with me and tease me about being nearly as skinny as that new model Twiggy was. I wondered what I'd look like if I had hair cut short as hers—maybe an animated scrub brush, I decided. I quailed at the thought.

Although Patty wanted to talk about it, I wasn't comfortable discussing the latest addition to the family even with her. Grace was having a hard time with her pregnancy. She got tired and out of breath easily and I had to help her a lot with the heavier tasks in the house. Always in the back of my mind was that coffin. It haunted me. Although my brothers and sisters expressed excitement about the new baby in their various ways, Georgie seemed the least excited. I think Georgie may have had a similar image in his mind, but it was hard to tell with Georgie. He was so quiet. I noticed that while Johnny tore about and made enough noise for both of them and terrorized the littler kids, he always put on gentler ways when Grace was around, and rushed to help her with carrying things. From time to time when he thought no one was looking, he watched her with a thoughtful look on his face. I wondered what he was thinking. Lanie and Janie seemed not to be worried. They just argued over who was going to hold the new baby the most and who the baby would love better.

I leafed desultorily through the magazine and then tossed it on the bed beside Patty, who looked up from the article she was reading.

"Tell you what, Patty. I have to watch Joey and the others for a while so Grace can rest, and you get the honor of helping me out. How's that sound?"

"Great!" She bounded off the bed and headed for the stairs. "Let's start now!"

Shaking my head at her enthusiasm, I followed her. The kids were downstairs in the kitchen. They seemed to live around that kitchen table these days. It was a favorite gathering place. Today Grace had put an old sheet over it and made a makeshift tent and the smaller ones were crawling in and out of the tent, fussing over who got to be in there and who didn't. I sighed and rolled my eyes. Patty, however, bent down and peered into the space created by the makeshift tent.

"Hi! Can I play?" She chirped, and climbed right in with the bunch of them, to their delight. They laughed and clapped their hands. For the next two hours she told them stories and played games with them, and crawled in and out as though she were no older than they were. She seemed to be enjoying herself immensely. I watched them play and peeled potatoes so that part of the meal would be done when Grace got up. I wished I could play with them like that. Once I had, but this last year had just taken my childhood clean out of me. I didn't have it in me to play.

When Grace came down from her nap to start supper, we had to take the sheet off the table. The little ones weren't happy, but were appeased by Patty's promise that she would come again, and they would make a tent, and it would be the biggest and best tent ever because it would be magic.

"Really," I teased her as we walked to the door when she was leaving, trailed by the little ones who were now devout Patty fans. "You take the cake. You'd think *you* were five."

"Sssh, Don't tell anyone. It's a secret. I'm the oldest five-year-old in the wooorrrrld," she replied. My little sisters and brothers giggled delightedly. Patty hugged each of them and turned to me. "Thanks, Annie! That was great."

"Maybe you'll make a good Aunt Patty after all!" I called after her as she left among a chorus of good-byes.

"Of course I will!"

CHAPTER TWENTY-ONE

Spring tip-toed in that year. Somewhere between the cold snaps, the trees began to put on their emerald coats, and in the fields, the emerging wheat covered the red dirt with a brilliant carpet of green. One day I heard a mockingbird singing his medley of greatest hits to a sky that was brilliantly blue, accompanied by a chorus of robins and sparrows and even a stray blue jay. Once I even saw a flash of scarlet among the row of trees lining the drive in our yard, a cardinal. Mama used to say that if you saw one of those, you would see someone you hadn't expected to see. I wished I could see *her.* I wondered if the birds missed the tree that had fallen. Its place created a space in the tree row that lined our drive that looked for all the world like one of the spaces left by a missing tooth in one of the twin's mouths.

I went every so often to Mama's grave, which was in the cemetery about a mile from our house. Going there didn't help me much. Some folks drew comfort in visiting their loved ones out in the cemetery, but I didn't. It just made the loss I felt even worse, because I knew she wasn't really there. I didn't like to think of her being there anyway. In my mind, she was in heaven, playing with the baby. Every now and then, I'd catch a glimpse of her in the tilt of Janie's head or in Georgie's shy smile. Every now and then, I'd swear she was just around the corner about to come into sight or just away on a journey and about to come home. Then the realization would hit and the pain that tore my heart would begin in earnest again. In my mind, our family was sort of like that row of trees. It had a big gap that no one could fill, especially not Grace, no matter how hard she tried.

As the days warmed, our classes at school were struck with spring fever. The teachers had a terrible time keeping our attention. We daydreamed, dawdled, or acted silly. The boys showed off and the girls giggled. The baseball team were our heroes. I went to the games as often as I could, not so much interested in the game, but in the opportunity to socialize and get my mind off things. Luke managed to show up when I did and sat with me, which made me wary, lest someone make something more of it than it was and report it to Daddy. I always tried to have Patty next to me in order to ward off the gossip.

Luke and I, after our confrontation, had fallen into an easy friendship, and he had finally talked about himself. He told me he was the youngest of three boys, and much younger than his next oldest brother—not quite an only child, but close. His mother and father were divorced and he lived with his dad. She lived in Tulsa, with his little sister by her current husband. Other than that, he was pretty closed-mouthed about it all. If I asked him anything he thought was nosy, he clammed up and changed the subject. That was my signal to quit, although I was eaten up with curiosity.

I told him about Mama's dying and how I had a step-mother. I told him about my brothers and sisters, and he laughed at my stories of their antics. He particularly liked the one when Johnny had let a mouse loose under Lanie's and Janie's feet. He said Johnny reminded him of himself when he was little. I told him I didn't believe he could ever have been as ornery as Johnny. He told me that yes, he had been, but he grew out of it. I told him I hoped Johnny would. He assured me he probably would. At the ball games he and Patty would spar at each other from either side of me. Sitting in the middle and letting their laughter and fun wash over me, I felt included and safe.

I didn't get to go to the games as often as I wanted though, because most of the time I was stuck helping Grace around the house. Daddy took a dim view of my socializing at the cost of helping Grace out with all the work she had to do. It was only right to help her, he said. There was too much work to do for one little woman who was carrying a baby. I didn't like to give up my social time, but a grudging sense of fairness that seemed to surface in me from time to time in spite of myself made me agree with him. That was a wonder since I didn't agree on anything about Grace with Daddy.

In addition to the unending round of work she did, Grace's sewing machine ran constantly now. She was making things for the baby. Daddy crawled up in the attic and brought down the well-used bassinet that I and my brothers and sisters all used in their turn. I was assigned the task of cleaning the dust off it and Grace made a new cover for it. I thought that was a waste of time since none of my brothers and sisters, as far as I knew, had ever slept well in it, but by now, I had learned to keep some of the things I thought to myself. Grace and I were getting along better as a result. I wouldn't say we were close, but we were managing. Daddy was relieved about not having to referee, I think. An uneasy truce, it was, but better than nothing, I guessed.

But as April drew nearer, I felt sadness descending on me like a huge, black cloak. Mama and the baby had died during the first part of the month. It was just one more, hard time to get through. I intended to get through it, if I had to cry my way through it. I had cried enough tears to raise the Washita River a foot, I thought. I would probably cry a few more. The hurt of Mama's absence was always present and my tears threatened to erupt in a geyser if there was the least opportunity to do so. I kept that grief tamped down as best I could, but I didn't always succeed. On those occasions I withdrew to my room, or if I were at school, I'd ask to be excused and flee to the restroom where I could cry in peace. I didn't like people to see me cry.

On the anniversary of her death, I went out to her grave in the cemetery and lay a bouquet of flowers on it. Daffodils had always been her favorite flower. I had raided the last of them from the garden and tied them with a pink ribbon. Someone else had been there and put roses at the base of the simple, granite headstone. I wondered if Daddy had been there, and what Grace thought of his going out there.

"Ella Ann Gibson," the granite stone read, "Beloved Wife and Mother." The baby's presence was acknowledged by the simple words, "Susanna, daughter of Ella and Thomas." I wondered what kind of person little Susanna would have grown up to be.

"I miss you, Mama. I love you," I said, turning away through another waterfall of tears. Try as I might, I could not find my Mama here. Here was simply more pain, and an emptiness I could not fill. If she were watching, I hoped she would understand why I didn't come to visit her grave more often. I wiped the tears away with a sleeve and stood up and turned to go.

I still struggled with feelings of resentment because Grace was there in Mama's place. Those feelings I stuffed down and tried not to let show. I had meant what I said about trying to keep my side of the peace. It wasn't easy. It was going to take a while to heal the large hole Mama's going had left in my heart, and the whole situation kept ripping the wound open over and over. I knew I shouldn't hate Grace, and I guess I didn't, but I didn't and couldn't love her. I didn't even want to try.

One warm day I slipped down to the creek to

my quiet spot. I hadn't been there since the last fall day that Patty had visited. I found Johnny there, sitting on the big, red rock that helped to define the riverbank, skipping stones out over the water. I slipped over and sat down beside him. His face was streaked with dirt and tears. I knew better than to ask him why he was crying. He would have been angry at my calling him on any sort of weakness.

I didn't need to ask anyway. I thought I knew. I sat there in silence beside him, figuring he would share if he wanted to, offering my presence as a kind of support. I hated to admit it, but Johnny was like me. He hated people to pry into his feelings and got all prickly when they did.

He skipped the last rock over the muddy red water and dusted his hands off. He didn't turn to look at me, but just sat there then, hands between his knees, and gazed into the water.

I looked around, drinking in the beauty that was this quiet spot. The wildflowers along the bank were beginning to bloom among the tall cottonwood trees by the waterside. The water, stained red from the mud on the banks, glistened and sparkled in the late morning sunlight. On an old piece of tree trunk nearby, a large turtle sat sunning itself, enjoying the early spring warmth. Overhead, beneath the arch of the blue spring sky, the birds in the trees scolded each other and us for disturbing them, and a hawk rode the currents of the soft breeze, looking for a stray field mouse. I hoped the mice knew to hide. I thought life was kind of like that hawk—always swooping in when you least expected it. I shivered in spite of the warmth.

Johnny and I sat for quite a while in silence. Absentmindedly, he bit at a hangnail and spit it out. I looked down at my hands, thought about biting my own hangnails, and that I really needed to do something about my bad habit, and waited for him to start the conversation. I had about given up on his doing so when he finally broke the silence.

"I really, really miss Mama," he said simply, wiping his nose with his sleeve.

"I know. I do too."

"You think we'll see her again someday like the preacher says?"

"We can hope to."

"You think Mama's in heaven?"

"I know so."

"Don't help us much down here does it?" A tear slipped out of the corner of his eye and rolled down his nose. He continued to stare out at the water, oblivious.

No it didn't, I thought. We were still here and hurting.

"Not really," I put my arm around him and we sat there for quite a while, drawing some comfort from the closeness. Johnny, the one who didn't like to be cuddled, leaned into me as I went on. "They tell me it gets easier. So far it hasn't. They tell me it takes time."

"How much time?"

"I don't know. Forever maybe. As long as it takes."

He leaned his head into my shoulder. I was overwhelmed with feelings of tenderness for him, this crazy little brother of mine with an attitude that was six feet tall. How could I help him when I couldn't help myself? I didn't even know how to try. I pulled him closer in the circle of my arms and lay my chin against his head.

We sat there for a while until he pulled away. His eyes, red with tears, regarded me dolefully. I reached up and ruffled his hair. "One thing I know though. We've got each other to help us pull through." My own tears were falling now. He reached out with a grubby finger and wiped a tear from my cheek.

"Thanks, Annie." He stood up and squared his shoulders. The sight of my tears and knowing that I shared his pain, seemed to have heartened him. Now he was anxious that no one knew he had given into it. "Don't tell anyone I was cryin', will ya?"

"Don't worry, I won't. I promise," He offered me his hand and helped me off the rock.

"Race you back to the house."

"You're on!" Leaving our tears behind, we sprinted away.

CHAPTER TWENTY-TWO

It was late afternoon. I was trying to do my homework, but I couldn't concentrate for the din that was happening.

"For Pete's sake, will you two girls stop it? I can't think!" I yelled. The twins were having one of their screeching fights again, and this one was threatening to become physical. I had been trying for half an hour to solve an equation for algebra in order to get ready for a test, but I kept getting the steps mixed up in my head, and their shrill argument made it almost impossible for me to get it sorted out.

"She has my color book!" Janie pointed to a dog-eared color book that Lanie was using. I didn't see how she knew which one was which since Grace had bought them identical books.

"Do not! It's *mine!*" Lanie put the book behind her back and stuck out her tongue at Janie.

"You broke my crayon too!" Janie wailed.

"Did not!"

"Did too!"

"Stop it! Give me the stupid book!" I grabbed it out of Lanie's grasp and held it above their heads while they both tried to jump to get it.

"Stop it, you hear? I'm sick of you two fighting. No one is going to color. Grace is trying to rest and I can't get my math done because you're making too much noise. Go outside and play!"

"You're mean!" Lanie informed me. "All you ever do is yell at us."

"I wonder why."

"I want my book back!" Janie tugged on my blouse, hard. I heard a seam rip.

"Now look what you did!" I raised my arm to survey the damage. "You ruined my blouse! Why do you have to be such brats? Why can't you ever behave?"

"I want my book back! I want my book back!"

"If you don't shut up I will throw it in the garbage!"

"You can't do that! It's *mine!*" Janie screamed.

Grace appeared in the doorway, "Janie! Lanie! Give me the color book and crayons, *now.*" She took the crayons from Lanie's hand and the coloring book from me. "Go to your room. I can't rest with all this shouting," she told the twins, who flounced off, probably to resume the war. I didn't care as long as they were away from me.

"I told them to pipe down," I said, as the girls flounced upstairs to our room.

"Just as loudly as they did," she said dryly. Her face was pale with fatigue. "I'm going back to bed for a little bit. Maybe you can get your homework done now."

"Doubt it. I don't get this stuff." I grumped.

Tutoring helped but I still struggled. Grace stifled a cross between a laugh and a yawn.

"Just keep working at it. You'll eventually get it if you try."

"Right. I've studied it all year and I'm still hopeless at it. Six weeks' tests are soon." I held my head in my hands despairingly.

She shook her head and turned and went back into the bedroom to lie down. I propped my chin on my hands and glared at the algebra book, as if it were my worst enemy. How I hated it! As soon as I got one thing, there would be something else even more complex to learn. It never ended. Giving up for the moment, I sighed and closed the book and drifted to the window. Through the panes, I could see Georgie sitting under one of the trees in the driveway, staring up at the sky. Georgie did that a lot. I wondered what he thought about. Giving up for the moment on understanding anything about the mysteries of math, I decided to go and join him. I made my way to where he was sitting and plopped down beside him.

"What you doing, Georgie?"

"Nothing." He picked up a stick and drew aimless lines in the dirt. "Just sitting."

"Can I join you?"

"Okay." He shrugged. I sat down beside him in the grass and put my arm around him. He stiffened, and then leaned into me, nestling.

"Feeling lonesome?"

"Yeah."

"Want to talk about it?"

He shrugged again. I looked up at the sky.

"It's all right if you don't. I just thought maybe you'd like some company, and I was kind of tired of doing math."

"Is it hard?"

"Yeah, to me it is. Patty says it's easy though.

"Oh." He made some small circles in the dirt with a stick and then looked up. He wiggled around so he could see my face. I could tell he was about to ask me something important. Georgie had an earnest little face and it was scrunched up now with the importance of what he had to say. Georgie spoke very little, but what he did say had a tendency to surprise people. I waited.

"Annie, do you think Mama's watching us right now?" he finally asked. "I was looking in the sky and hoping she was looking down from one of those clouds there."

"I don't know, Georgie," I struggled to keep the tears that were always there threatening to fall at the mention of Mama "She might be."

"But I can't see her," he said solemnly. "I've been looking all afternoon."

"Oh, Georgie," I hugged him hard. "Mama's too far off for us to see with our eyes."

"She is?"

"I'm afraid so," I answered.

"Then how can she see us?"

I had no answer for that. When I was little, I used to think the angels walked around on the clouds and I used to wonder how they kept from falling off. The clouds, when I was small had been solid things to me, capable of bearing weight. I had learned better in science class. Maybe the angels didn't need clouds to be solid. Sighing, I held Georgie close and together we watched the white, puffy, late-afternoon clouds waltz across the sky. Maybe somewhere up on one of those puffy clouds, Mama was dancing.

I told Georgie that. It seemed to comfort him.

CHAPTER TWENTY-THREE

Easter came that year in a flurry of pink organdy dresses for the little girls, slacks and vests and white shirts and pomaded hair for all the little boys and an almost-grown-up yellow silk dress for me, *a la* Jackie Kennedy, the former first lady that I admired. Grace had outdone herself even though the effort took a lot out of her. She was determined that we look especially presentable on this particular Sunday. She insisted that I also wear white gloves and carry a folded handkerchief in my Bible, and that I wear hose, in spite of my protests. I hated those things, and the things that held them up were uncomfortable too. I argued and fussed, but she was adamant. Ladies wore hose to church, especially on Easter. I gave in when she told me others would be saying things if I didn't. How I hated to be gossiped about, and if this was one thing I could prevent as an occasion for gossip, I was all for it.

Grace herself was resplendent in a green lace dress with a matching lace jacket that reached to the hem of the dress and minimized her pregnancy. A pill-box hat sat on top of her carefully coiffed hair that she had managed to tame from its usual frizziness. She too wore white gloves. Daddy had a new, dark blue suit for the occasion. It must have taken a special effort to get him back into a suit after the wedding. He swore then he didn't want to wear another until they buried him.

After a huge flurry of effort to get everyone presentable, Grace and Daddy shooed us out the door, and we all piled into the station wagon for the ride to our church. We were headed out early so we could get a seat in the service and sit together. Usually we grabbed a seat wherever we could if Daddy and Grace weren't with us. Sometimes they sent us with others and those didn't care where we sat. I preferred the back row, and Johnny and Georgie usually sat with me. When we all went, Janie and Lanie usually sat one on a side of Grace and Daddy. Dividing and conquering, Daddy called it. I called it a pain in the neck. The boys' wiggling and acting up were distracting. They were acting up now as we rode to church. I would have preferred to ride in another vehicle, if one had been available. As it was, I gritted my teeth and suppressed the urge to slap them silly.

Right after Grace and Daddy had gotten married, they had started going to church, although not regularly. On the occasions that they did go, Grace didn't seem to notice or mind the stares people directed at her and Daddy, but sat quietly, in her usual Grace-like way, face turned to the front of the auditorium. She answered any nosy questions politely, without encouraging any more of them. I didn't know how she did it. The stares and whispered conversations made me squirm. It was the reason I always sat on the back row whenever I came alone, and I usually managed to slip out to avoid anyone bent on asking questions. I hadn't escaped in time once, and it had been unpleasant. I didn't have Grace's finesse, and I managed to offend the questioner, who promptly reported that I had been rude. Daddy had listened politely. Once the irate woman had gone, he merely told me not to be impolite and left it at that. I guess he knew I had my reasons.

We got there early enough to find a pew that would seat all of us and sat down, spreading the little ones out among us. No dividing and conquering this morning, I thought as I poked Johnny in the ribs as a reminder to sit up straight. I didn't know how anyone was going to listen to the sermon. I was sure that it was going to be an all-out battle. To my surprise, however, the little ones were pretty good. Bobby caused a few looks and smiles to be directed our way by singing loudly off key during the hymns. He snuggled up to Daddy's side, and Joey curled up on Daddy's shoulder and both went to sleep, Joey sucking his thumb. Johnny was even fairly well behaved. Georgie sat quietly at my side, his solemn face lifted towards the cross hanging above the choir loft. The little girls were arranged on either side of Grace, who kept a protective arm around each of them and bent time to time to hear what they were saying. Even having to keep an eye on Johnny, I managed to hear a little bit of what the preacher was saying. He was preaching a sermon on unconditional love. I listened with half an ear since Johnny was showing signs of restlessness. He hated sitting still for long, and he wasn't really good about listening. I was relieved when the service ended, and he hadn't caused any major disturbance, which would have embarrassed me no end.

We were gathering our things up to go and hadn't left the pew when Birdie Jones came bearing down on us. Birdie was one of those women who just have to be in everyone's business. When people around town said that a little birdie told them something, they usually meant her. I look one look at her large, floral figure, iron gray hair, and the determined expression in her beady, black eyes, and knew we were in for it. Birdie didn't talk to anyone unless she could dig out some scandal to broadcast about town, and she made sure it was broadcast. In her eyes we were fair game. I thought I would have an awful hard time feeling unconditional love for this woman. I stood warily as she stopped in the middle of the empty pew, the other occupants having left hurriedly when they saw her heading in their direction. *Lucky!* I thought.

"Well I declare! If it isn't the Gibsons! I haven't seen you all together like this in a long time! Ann Marie, you are just getting to be a beautiful young lady! And look at all these lovely children!" Her voice was syrupy sweet as she bent to look at Bobby, who was peering at her from behind the safety of Daddy's leg.

I suppressed the urge to make a really ugly face at her.

"And so beautifully dressed too! How do you ever manage on a carpenter's salary?" She breathed wonderingly.

Old cat! What business is it of yours? I fumed. It was none of her business about how we got new clothes. Grace had her own money, and it was out of this that she had purchased the material for the new dresses and little suits that she had made herself. It was something Grace didn't talk about or flaunt for fear of hurting Daddy's feelings. She would dip into it from time to time to provide us with little extras, but she was always careful not to do too much. I imagined Birdie Jones would have a field day with that information.

"We manage," Grace said politely, but coolly, as we maneuvered out of the pew past Birdy. "Isn't it amazing what you can do with Green Stamps? Please excuse us, we have a commitment," She murmured as a parting shot, leaving Birdy to gape at her as she and Daddy and I made a big business of gathering up the children and beat a hasty retreat. I grabbed Johnny by his collar and dragged him, protesting, after me. *Let her have something to say about that!* I thought. *For that matter, she could have Johnny. It would serve her right!*

When we were in the car, Daddy laughed until he wiped the tears from his eyes. "Did you see her face? That was really funny. You really put her in her place!"

"I don't know if her kind can ever be put in their places," Grace said, looking straight ahead. "She may deal me some misery over it. No telling what she'll make up to say."

"Well, she's an old misery herself anyway. Everyone knows what she is," I said.

"Now, Annie, I don't want you to talk disrespectfully of your elders, even if they deserve it," Daddy started the car, chuckling.

Grace just sighed, leaned back, and closed her eyes, hands resting on her rounded tummy.

"I'll tell you what! Let's go for a little drive," Daddy said. The kids chorused their enthusiasm.

Oh goody, a drive with these little heathens, I told myself and shrank back into the corner formed by the seat and the door to put as much space as possible between me and Johnny, who was no doubt thinking up some revenge for being collared.

"I think we'll go see Nannie and Grandpa Smith. I think they'll get a kick out of seeing how handsome their grandkids are. I called ahead and they are expecting us. How's that sound to you, Sweetheart?" He said to Grace, who smiled at him in delight.

Sweetheart! He used to call Mama that, I thought with a pang. The pleasure I had in the sunny day and the besting of Birdie Jones receded as I fought to contain my resentment. It seemed that every time I got over one thing, something else cropped up to hurt me. I turned my face to the green landscape racing by, and fought the bitterness that threatened to well up in me like a sudden Oklahoma thunderstorm.

I didn't say much during the drive. I didn't like going to Grace's parents' house. I didn't think they liked me much anyway. To me, the ride was a misery. We kids were packed in like sardines, even in the station wagon, with everyone complaining because everyone else was touching them. Johnny was busy trying to poke at Lanie's ears just to hear her shriek and complain and Janie was singing off-key to Bobby, who joined in and was giggling wildly. Georgie and I were the only quiet ones. I wondered where on earth we would put the baby when it came. Maybe I could stay home, I thought hopefully.

I entertained myself with the notion of Daddy's buying a school bus to carry us all. The thought amused me the rest of the way. I pictured it being painted green, and my brothers and sisters hanging out the windows. I could see that happening. What I couldn't see happening, was my arriving in style on that bus. It would be worse than the one I rode to school. My thoughts were interrupted by Johnny's flicking me on the ear. Irritated, I slapped his hand away. Lanie and Janie were now singing their ABC's, each interrupting the other over who was correctly singing it. Joey, who had woken up, and was cranky was whining, and Bobby was bouncing up and down in the seat. I was glad Grandpa and Nannie didn't live in the next state. I didn't think I would survive without opening the door and jumping out.

They were all still rowdy when we piled out of the station wagon in front of the two-story house that Grace's parents owned. They had a really nice place. The house was red brick with white-shuttered windows and trim, and it had a big wrap-around porch, supported by brickwork pillars and square white columns. A wide sidewalk from the circle drive led to the porch. Everything was kept trim and neat. Even the grass stopped at the edge of the sidewalk as though trained to do so. Rockers adorned the porch, which was as clean swept as any inside room, and pots of geraniums, placed outside to take advantage of the warm, early spring sunshine, sat at either end of the steps. Nannie Smith liked everything orderly and neat. It must have been a trial to her when we visited, and the little ones managed to break something or spill something. She never let on that she minded though. I had to give her that.

On the north side of the house, a big red barn with a grain silo vied with the house for attention. Whenever we visited, the boys usually had a ball playing in it, although I didn't know how much they would get to today since they were dressed in church clothes. At first, Daddy had gotten on to them for going into the barn, but Grandpa Smith had said to leave them alone and let them have fun. He said that unless they fell on their heads, there wasn't anything in there to hurt them, unless you counted the hay. Since then, the barn had become the boys' hangout, and they had a good time climbing the wood stanchions and exploring every nook and cranny of it. I envied them. I wished I was still young enough to climb all over everything. Maybe the visits here wouldn't bore me so much then.

Grace's parents came out on the porch when they heard the car. Nannie Smith ran to the car door and opened it and leaned in to hug Grace, clucking over her paleness, and insisted she lie down until the noon meal was ready, while leading her into the house with an arm around her shoulders. Grandpa Smith and Daddy trailed off to the barn with all the bigger kids and Bobby in tow, leaving me standing in the middle of the yard with Joey in my arms. Reluctantly, I followed the two women into the house.

Although they had always been good to me, I didn't feel comfortable around either of Grace's parents. I felt they were always judging me, especially Nannie Smith, who always was asking me to tuck my shirt in my skirt or to stop biting my nails. I felt, sometimes, that she was looking for things to find fault with. Both Nannie and Grandpa knew the problems that Grace and I had had, and, although they didn't say anything, I was sure they disapproved of me.

I wandered into the spotlessly-kept living room and sat down in the rocker by the fireplace. Joey snuggled sleepily against me and I wrapped my arms around him and held him tightly and rocked him. I hummed an old lullaby that Mama had hummed to me when I was little. When he was older, I would tell him that. At least he would have that for a memory of Mama, I thought fiercely.

I wondered if Grace would treat him any differently once her baby came. Right now, she treated the little ones pretty well, but maybe her own would make a difference in her feelings. I stared down at the dozing baby in my arms, considering the possibility. Nannie Smith bustled in and brought a blanket to put on the floor for a pallet. I thanked her and laid him down, careful not to wake him. She went on into the kitchen to finish Sunday dinner.

"Ann Marie, can you come and help me peel the potatoes, please?" She called as she looked into the oven to check on the ham that was baking. "I declare! It's a good thing I put this ham in this morning. Had a feeling I was going to have company, and when your daddy called, I knew I was right."

"Yes, Ma'am," I trailed into the kitchen. Apparently I wasn't going to get out of peeling potatoes, even here, even in my Sunday clothes. I washed my hands at the sink and looked up to find her regarding me appraisingly. She handed me an apron, and I put it on.

"Grace says you've been a big help to her," Nannie said.

"Guess so," I shrugged and picked up the knife to peel the potatoes she was laying out for me to peel. "I try, anyway."

"Well, I appreciate what you do,"

"Thank you." I went on peeling potatoes, eyes lowered. While I was finishing the peeling and cutting them up to put in the large pot she had set out to boil them in, she finished getting other things to cook onto the stove. Nannie, I had discovered during one of the visits, loved to can vegetables and fruits from the garden she and Grandpa kept and the orchard that stood behind the barn. She had drafted me to help her with it. I discovered I didn't like canning. I also discovered that, although I didn't care for canning I didn't mind eating the finished projects in the meals that were subsequently served.

She worked efficiently and quickly, with brisk movements. She and Grace didn't resemble each other at all. Where Grace was thin, she tended towards plumpness. Her graying hair was raked tightly back from her rounded face into a bun at the back of her neck, and she had bright blue eyes. The softness of her figure and face belied her no-nonsense personality. I was sure she would make a good general. I was careful to peel the potatoes with as little waste as possible. I was sure she would pounce if I didn't. The last time, she had.

Grandpa Smith was a different story. He was always joking and never seemed to be in a hurry about anything. He didn't look like Grace much either, except for those light gray eyes. Even though he joked a lot, he seemed to observe and weigh people. Sometimes I caught him looking at me with that measuring glance, although he was careful to smile when I caught him. I kind of thought he didn't like much what he saw. It made me uncomfortable. He seemed to like my brothers and sisters well enough, though.

They adored him and followed him around like puppies. He took them to feed the calves and the little ones had a ball feeding the calves from the galvanized pails with nipples attached. He seemed to find everything they did vastly amusing, and I heard him belly laugh often over something that Johnny had come up with. He had an easy relationship with Daddy, who seemed to respect any advice he gave. I guessed I was just the oddball.

I finished peeling the potatoes and gave them to Nannie. Once everything was on the stove, Nannie Smith slipped upstairs with a glass of cold lemonade to check on Grace. I tiptoed into the living room to check on Joey, who was still sound asleep, then I started up the stairs to go to the bathroom.

I was washing up when their voices stopped me cold. Grace was talking. I hesitated, straining my ears to hear what was said.

"I am so very, very tired."

"I know, honey." Nannie's voice was tender and soothing, quite different from her normal way of speaking.

"You just don't know what it's like. I work and I work and I work and now..."

"It will be all right. Your condition just makes it seem worse."

"Another baby, how will I cope?"

"Well honey, you knew what you were getting into, and if you didn't, well Dad and I tried to tell you."

"I thought I knew, but I didn't. Every day I live with the ghost of another woman in the house and I feel like I can't live up to her, no matter what I do."

"Does Tom actually say that?" Nannie's

voice sounded indignant.

I clenched my teeth. Daddy had never said a word to her in my presence.

"No, he has been the soul of goodness to me, but I feel it. I see it every now and then. He gets a sad, faraway look in his eyes, and then I *know* he's thinking about her," Grace's voice was fretful.

Good for Daddy! I thought.

"That's only natural, honey. I would want Henry to think of me if I were gone. "

"That's just it. I can't compete with a ghost, and then there's Annie."

All right, here it comes, I thought. *At last I'll know what she really thinks of me at least.*

"What about her?" Nannie Smith asked. "She seems helpful and polite."

"To you," Grace said bitterly. "To me, she's rude and ungracious, and she never lets me forget for a single moment that she isn't my daughter. Oh, she has tried to get along lately, and there are moments when she is almost pleasant, but I have to walk on eggshells around her."

Her words burned into me as I stood there on the stairs. My anger mounted as Grace went on, "I can't count the times I've had to bite my tongue and overlook the things she's said. I don't even feel like I can talk to Thomas about her because I don't want to come between them, and when I do say something, they fight and fight. It's like living in a war zone with her all the time."

I had heard enough. I fled down the stairs, and out the door, slamming it as I went. Joey woke and wailed, but I didn't stop to see about him. Daddy and Grandpa Smith were standing in the yard.

"I want to go home!" I yelled.

"For Pete's sake, Annie," What's wrong with you?

"Take me home! I don't want to be here."

Daddy's face went from puzzlement to startled anger. "Now, Annie, that's no way to act," he warned. I was angry enough to disregard the warning.

"I don't care!"

Nannie Smith came into the yard with a snuffling Joey, wide-eyed in her arms. "What on earth has gotten into the child? She slammed the door and woke this little mite up. She was fine when I left the kitchen."

"Maybe you shouldn't talk about me behind my back!" I yelled. I took off down the drive.

"Annie! You come back here and apologize." Daddy called after me in his sternest voice.

"Won't!" I yelled.

"Let her go, Tom," Grandpa Smith said. I looked over my shoulder to see that he had placed a hand on Dad's shoulder. "Whatever it is, she's too mad to listen to you right now anyway. She'll simmer down after a while," I heard him say.

"Here, take the baby," Nanny Smith said. "I've got dinner to see to." She handed Joey to Grandpa and went back into the kitchen. "I don't have time to deal with her."

Just like that. No apology. No nothing. Just, "I've got dinner to see to." It made me even madder. Obviously my feelings weren't of importance. I went stomping down the drive to the

road and kept on going, leaving Daddy and
Grandpa to stare after me.

CHAPTER TWENTY-FOUR

I stomped halfway to the next section line before I settled down. I would have cut across a pasture, but there was a large, brown bull staring at me quizzically. I was tired and sweaty and hot, and my shoes were beginning to hurt my feet. Now that I was calmer, I wondered what was going to happen as a result of my angry outburst. It didn't matter, I told myself fiercely. I was tired of everything. Let them send me away. I didn't care anymore. I sat down by the fence row, heedless of the condition of my dress, and wrapped my arms around my knees. What now? I did *not* want to go back there, and I was darned if I was going to apologize to anyone. Hadn't I been trying lately? Guess that didn't count for anything. As for coming between Daddy and me, I was sure *she* already had. I rested my chin on my knees and stared at a lone ant making its way through the grass beside the road. Bet that ant knew how I felt. It was all alone too.

I'd been there long enough to get tired of sitting when I heard the chug of a vehicle coming down the road. I got up, prepared to take out across the field and chance the bull's attentions if it were Daddy. It wasn't. It was Grandpa Smith. I watched his approach warily, ready to run.

He pulled up beside me and leaned out the window.

"Want a lift?

"Not really."

"Well, I figured as how you wanted to go home so bad that you'd take out walking in this heat, I better come get you before anything happened to you. Your dad is fit to be tied."

"I'm fine," I said stiffly. Actually I wasn't. I didn't want to back and face Daddy's wrath though.

"Long way home."

"Well I'm not going back *there*."

"Well you can't walk home either. You aren't thinking straight."

"Straight enough to know when I'm not wanted."

He gave a surprised little huff, "Is that what you think?

"It's what I know."

He regarded me steadily for a few minutes. I looked down at my shoes. My dress shoes were liberally coated with dirt. I hoped I could get all the dirt off. I was aware of the sweat trickling down the back of my neck. I wiped it off with an impatient swipe of my hand.

Grandpa Smith cleared his throat. "If I promise not to take you right back, will you get in and let me at least talk to you? I think it's time we had a conversation."

I wasn't in any mood for conversation, but he

was right. It was a long way home and I couldn't walk it. Maybe I could talk him into taking me home and then I could leave before the rest got home. I'd have time since he'd have to drive all the way back and tell them that he found me, and then they had to drive home. That ought to be time enough to get away. I'd go to Grandma and Grandpa Jenkins house, I thought. They and daddy could fight it out over whether I could stay. With that in mind, I mumbled, "I guess."

Grandpa Smith pushed the rider's side door of the pickup open and I climbed in. To his credit, he didn't fuss at me when I slammed the door a little harder than I needed to.

We rode in silence for a good stretch of road. To my surprise he went on to the next section line and turned south. When I asked him where we were going, he told me we were taking the long way home so I could cool down. We rode in silence until he turned back east at the next road. Then he said, "What happened back there that made you so mad?

I stared out at the passing countryside. "It was Grace and Nannie. They were talking about how bad I was."

"Oh?"

"I don't like people talking behind my back."

"Guess I don't either," he said. "How'd you know they were talking about *you*?"

"I heard them. Pretty hard to miss when they say your name."

"Hmmm."

"Grace was telling Nannie how rude and

disrespectful I was and how it was like living in a war zone with me,"

He didn't respond to that, and I continued to stare out the window. I didn't figure that he would under-stand, Grace's being his daughter. After a few minutes, he stopped the truck, turned to me and sighed heavily. I stared straight ahead, waiting for him to speak.

"You know, I tried to tell Grace how it would be, but she loved your Daddy and was set on marrying him. I told her that she would have a lot to deal with. Kids that have lost their mom weren't going to take real kindly to a replacement."

"*No one* can replace my Mama!" I told him fiercely, turning to face him. "No one!"

"See? But she thought she could give you lots of love and sort of make up for the loss. What she didn't understand was that maybe you didn't want it."

"I don't."

"Then why does what she said hurt so bad?" He shifted gears and we started forward again. "Seems to me like an awful lot of fuss, if you don't care about her."

I didn't know. I didn't know what to make of this man either. Here he was the father of the woman I resented most in the world, and he seemed to understand my feelings. He hadn't condemned me for feeling the way I did. On the other hand, he hadn't condemned his daughter either. He started the truck again, and we drove to the next road going back north, the old Chevy wheezing and sputtering as we switched gears.

"Can I ask you something?" He said after his words had had a chance to do their work. "Who are you really mad at? Your daddy for marrying Grace, Grace for marrying your daddy? Your Mama for dying?"

I didn't answer for a moment, but then I burst out, "I'm mad at all of them. Mama for going and leaving me and Daddy for not caring and marrying someone right away and Grace for trying to take her place." The tears were rolling down my face.

"Well, until you get over that mad spell, you won't be able to see that you are welcome at my home, and that the wife and I kind of like our new grandkids. Never thought we'd have but one or two and we have a whole herd now." He fished in his overall pocket and handed me a clean, folded bandanna. "Here, blow your nose and wipe your eyes."

"I don't know how to get over it," I said dismally, taking the bandanna and mopping at my eyes and sniffing. "I just can't get around it, no matter how hard I try."

"Guess it will take a while," looking both ways, he eased the old pickup onto the road that led back to his house.

"How long?" I remembered Johnny's asking the same question. There, maybe Grandpa could answer it.

"Long as it takes, I guess. I hope it just doesn't take too long, for all your sakes," he sighed heavily.

I started to hand him back the bandanna. At that, he grinned and said, "You can keep it."

I looked down at the soggy mess that had been his clean bandanna, and laughed in spite of myself.

"Oh, guess you don't want it back now."

"Not too fond of tears and snot," He winked at me.

"Grandpa Smith?"

"Uh huh?"

"I'm sorry."

"Me too. Never thought you didn't feel welcome. Not true you know."

"Guess Nannie won't want me back."

"Bet she does," He laughed. "Wouldn't be the first time we had to deal with a temper fit. Grace used to throw some good ones. She did at that. We didn't think we were going to survive, but we did," he chuckled.

I was trying to picture the self-controlled Grace throwing fits. Imagination failed me.

"Why did you come after me instead of Daddy's doing it?"

"As I said, he was pretty wound up. Anyways, would you have let him talk to you?"

"Probably not." I stared glumly out the window. "I'm in for it now."

"Probably. He's pretty upset, and embarrassed that you acted that way. You still want to go home? I would like to eat my dinner first, and I think you could probably eat too."

"I don't know what I want to do now," I admitted. "I just hope Daddy will let me do it when I decide."

"What were you going to do?"

"I was going to go home and pack my things and leave. I was going to see if I could go to my grandma's house or go live with one of my aunts or something and never come back again."

"Hmmm. Never is a long time not to see your brothers and sisters, no matter how mad you are at your Daddy and Grace."

"I guess so," I stared out the window, bleakly. He had a point. "Yeah,"

"So what are you going to do? Go away forever, or make peace?"

"According to Grace, I'm the cause of living in a war. I've been trying to be peaceful. I really have. It's just hard…"

"Yup, I can see that."

"But if I go back to your house now, I'll be embarrassed to face Nannie, and then Daddy will be so mad at me he can't see straight, and I'll get blamed for making him look bad in front of you."

"We already talked that out. He allowed as how you are having a hard time with all of this stuff. Grace admitted she had said things and apologized to your dad. As for making him look bad to me, it doesn't, and when he apologized, I told him to stop blaming himself. A man caught between two women is in a terrible place. As for Nannie, a good apology goes a long way. Now I'm not a preaching man, but I am going to tell you one thing. Going away angry is not a good thing. Forever is a long time. You think about that."

I stared at the balled up bandana in my hand. Much as I didn't want to admit it, he had a point. Did I really want to go away forever? I was going to have to face Daddy sometime. It might as well be now. I squared my shoulders determinedly. I might as well get it over with.

"Grandpa? Can we go back to your house now?"

"That's what I was hoping you'd say! I thought I was going to have to drive right on past the driveway and miss my dinner. This fat man is hungry."

His eyes met mine, not at all judgmental as I had thought, and, in spite of myself and the predicament I was in, I laughed.

No one came out when we pulled up to the house. Inside we found them sitting at the table, filled plates before them.

"We were hungry, and didn't know when you'd be back," Nannie said calmly to Grandpa as he seated himself, and she handed him the mashed potatoes. Turning to me, she said, "Go wash your face and hands, Annie. You look a sight."

I fled to the bathroom to repair what damage I could. She was right. I washed my sweaty face and hands and tried to make myself look a little more presentable. A lot of good it did.

Daddy and Grace avoided looking at me. He still had a mad look on his face, sort of like a big, gray thunderhead before the storm hit. I wondered how he'd looked before Grandpa Smith talked to him. He must have looked even worse. Grace was picking at her food as though it were the worst tasting thing in the world. I slipped into my seat and helped myself to the food that Nannie pressed upon me. I guess she felt that a little food wouldn't hurt anything. I didn't have much appetite. I picked at my food, waiting for the axe of Daddy's anger to fall. The little ones eyed me sideways. They were uncharacteristically quiet.

"Now eat. We'll sort things out when we are done," Grandpa said, and tucked into his food with gusto. "Things are always better on a full stomach."

Johnny kicked me under the table. I turned to give him a piece of my mind, but the look on his face stopped me. It was troubled. Georgie and the twins stared at their plates as they ate. They knew I was in trouble and were waiting to see what would happen. It was never a good idea to sass Daddy. I could tell they were worried about what he would do.

We finished our meal in a strained silence. I figured Daddy would call me into another room and let me have it once we were done, but he surprised me. He did call me in, but instead of yelling, I was met with a cold silence when I ventured to say I was sorry. Grace stood tensely by his side, twisting her hands, and then put her hand on his arm. He shook it off, glared at me a moment, and then turned on his heel and left. Grace and I were left to stare at each other uncomfortably.

"Well, I'm in for it now," I muttered.

"Annie..." the words were soft, tentative, "I never meant..."

"Well, you did. I shouldn't have yelled at Daddy, but you made me so mad with what you said."

"I only spoke truth, and I never meant you to overhear. Am I not allowed to talk to my own mother about how I'm feeling?" Her tone was harder now.

"And you feel like that?" I crossed my arms, ready to do battle.

"Yes, yes…I do," She said after a minute, face averted. "I feel that no matter what I do to reach you, you are going to slap it down, and if you are honest with me, you'd admit it." She sat down in the chair as though all the air had gone out of her. "If I tell your dad how you are acting, he gets too angry with you and then blames us both for not getting along. I've taken and taken and taken your rudeness, but I have feelings too."

I went to the window and looked out. Daddy was sitting on the porch with his head down and his shoulders slumped. It made me feel bad. I turned.

"Can I really be honest with you, Grace? "

"I thought you already had been. I feel quite beaten up with all the honesty," she said coldly. I stared, this wasn't the patient Grace I had been used to dealing with. Maybe Grandpa Smith hadn't been telling tales.

"Now I'm going to be honest with you," she went on. "You've been punishing me for marrying your dad, and being as rude to me as you can be because I dared to love him. I thought, however mistakenly, I could maybe make up to you children for your loss." She laughed bitterly, and when I started to answer her, put her hand up. "No, don't. You've behaved like a brat, and I've put up with more from you than I would ever put up from anyone because you lost your mother, but I won't any more. I told your dad that already. As you daily remind me, I'm not your mother. Contrary to what you think, I never wanted to take her place in yours or anyone's heart. You walk around with your attitude and your ways, and you act like you are the only one in the world who is hurting, and because of that you hurt everyone around you. I don't even know why I care what you think anymore, but I do."

Not knowing how to face her anger, I turned to go. She put her hand on my shoulder and turned me around to face her. I stared at her in surprise as she went on, gray eyes glinting with anger.

"Go ahead and run out that door just like you always do. Make everyone chase you. You make your dad feel like he has done something wrong every time you run off. Did you know that? I apologized to him for voicing my feelings to my own mother in what I thought was a private conversation that you had no problem listening in on. But you hear this: I am not sorry I said them." She brushed past me and went back out to the kitchen.

I stood there while her hot words washed around and through me and scalded me. Anger and resentment warred with the part of my conscience that said she was speaking the truth. Fine, I thought glumly. Daddy wasn't speaking to me and Grace had just put me in my place. It wasn't a comfortable place at all.

CHAPTER TWENTY-FIVE

We drove home from Nannie and Grandpa Smith's that night in silence. Nannie had graciously accepted my apology. Grandpa had wrapped me in a hug and whispered in my ear, "This too shall pass."

It didn't. Daddy was still in a cold rage as we drove home. Grace was silent. Once home, he told me to get out of the car and go to my room. He told me I could not go out of my room, except to do chores, for a month, and at the end of that time, we would see whether or not I could treat him and Grace with respect. The girls would bunk downstairs on the couch bed, he said. His cold demeanor hurt me more than any spanking. The worst part was that he didn't get over the coldness as time passed. He spoke curtly to me when I tried to talk to him, and otherwise acted as though I didn't exist. I think that hurt me more than anything he could have done. I was sure I had lost my Daddy once and for all.

After her outburst, Grace treated me with an unfailing courtesy that made me even more uncomfortable. She seemed determined not to lose her temper with me again. I was careful to be polite in return. Neither of us referred to that day at her parents, for fear of stirring up things again. We circled around each other like two strange dogs, each wary of the other.

School was the only outlet from the tensions at home, but apparently the teachers decided we weren't doing enough work. I came home with piles of homework. It made me almost glad for the house arrest of my bedroom. At least I had peace and quiet, although with the penalty imposed by Daddy, I couldn't have Patty over to help me with the algebra. She had rolled her eyes when I told her of my punishment and, un-Patty-like, had no comment on what had caused it.

"Well, I hope you are off restriction by the end of the month," she said. 'I had hopes that you would be able to go on an outing with my parents and me to the zoo."

"The zoo?"

"Yeah, I know. My parents still think I'm a little kid," she laughed. "I think it would be fun if you got to go with me. I might even talk them into taking us to Spring Lake."

"That would be great!"

"Then you better be good."

"I hope Daddy will let me go."

"I do too. Oh look at what Sally has on! Really, it looked better on Twiggy."

Trust Patty to make me laugh. I hurried into history and sat down with only a moment to spare. Mr. Trent eyed me, but didn't make a remark. I was thankful. The last time I had come in late, he had gotten on to me, and the class and I were treated to a lecture about being on time. I didn't want to go through that again.

Luke didn't say much when he was told I was grounded. We wouldn't be sitting together at any more ball games, that was for sure. He continued to walk me back and forth between classes. I was grateful for his silent acceptance. He didn't pry. That was restful.

The days of my punishment wore on. Daddy continued to treat me like a stranger. It grieved me. In the solitude of my room, I lay on my stomach across the bed and brooded. In my own self-pity, I didn't notice that he was treating Grace the same way, or that she often looked after him with a sorrowful expression. One day I did, though, and to my surprise, it made me even sadder. I should have felt satisfaction. I didn't. What I felt was dismay. I didn't say anything though. This new quiet, cold Daddy was one I didn't know, and the last time I had opened my mouth to him, it had resulted in my winding up alone in my room.

Grace never let on to any of us that things weren't going well between her and Daddy. She continued to do all the things she could, but she asked for my help as little as possible. Out of guilt, I began to do extra things for her whenever I could, after my imprisonment in my room ended. It seemed like I was the only one that saw the still, sorrowful expression that settled on her face from time to time. She always put on a smile when dealing with the little ones though.

When my punishment ended, the girls moved

back into my room. They were glad to be back, they told me. They were tired of sleeping on the couch bed. It was lumpy, they said. They proceeded to pester me to the point that it almost made me wish I were alone again. I had actually missed them, though, and surprised myself at being happy they were there.

To my surprise, in spite of his distance, Daddy told me I could go with Patty and her parents on their trip. I wondered if he wanted me out of his hair, but stifled the thought. I wasn't going to let things interfere with my enjoyment of the trip. Her parents had agreed to take us to both the zoo and the amusement park. Johnny was outspoken in his envy.

"You're gonna get to ride the Big Dipper! I hear it's really scary! Wish I could go!"

"Well, you can't, but I'll see if I can bring you something."

I was heading out the door with my suitcase when Grace called to me. She tucked something into my hand and told me to have a good time. When I got in the car, and opened my palm, I saw a twenty-dollar bill. Dumbfounded, I stared through the window at her as we pulled away. Patty couldn't believe it.

"Wow! You're rich! That'll buy you a lot of hamburgers and cokes!" she said. "That was really generous of her."

"Yeah," I murmured, staring at the wadded up bill, "It was." I wondered why she had done it. Twenty dollars was a lot of money! I decided to spend it on souvenirs for the little ones.

Our trip to the zoo was memorable. Patty insisted that I was down there, clambering around with the other monkeys in the monkey pit on the mock-up of a half-submerged ship, and I told her I saw one that looked like her too. She made monkey noises at me, which caused those around us to laugh. For once I didn't care if someone did laugh. We were having a really good time.

We strolled through the various zoo exhibits and sat on the grass by the small lake and generally enjoyed ourselves, even though the late spring day was humid and hot. Patty's parents laughed and joked along with us. They even rode some of the rides when we went to Spring Lake, although they drew the line at riding the Big Dipper, which Patty and I rode over and over after we nearly scared ourselves to death the first time. I spent some of the money Grace had given me on mementos for my brothers and sisters, and stuffed myself on cotton candy and popcorn.

We feasted our eyes, as well, on the boys who were there, giggling and poking one another and acting silly, terrified that one of them might actually notice us and talk to us. Her parents looked on, vastly amused and indulgent. I drank in the experiences thirstily.

I had mentioned to Patty's mom that Aunt May lived in Oklahoma City, so she took us to see Aunt May while we were there. Aunt May was surprised and delighted to see us. She took us out to her covered, back-garden patio, which was surrounded by all sorts of colorful flowers and fed us lunch at the picnic table, all the while exclaiming how very happy she was that we had dropped by.

Her keen eyes assessed me as I hugged and kissed her in greeting and settled myself in a patio chair. She didn't come right out and ask anything about home, but I think she wondered how things were going. I was surprised when Patty's mom drew me aside and asked if I would like to visit with my aunt while she and Patty called on some people they knew. I told her I would. With a promise to be back around five, Patty and her mom left.

They were barely out the door, before Aunt May began peppering me with questions. How were things? How was school? How were the kids? How was I?

"Fine, Aunt May, really."

"I can tell by your voice they aren't. What's going on?"

I opened my mouth to tell her that things were fine again, but my voice deserted me, and I couldn't answer.

"Ann Marie. You be honest now. You want to talk about it, honey?"

Haltingly I began to tell her about the day Grace and I had the big fight. Aunt May shook her head throughout the telling, but didn't comment much. I told her about Daddy and how he treated Grace and me now, and how Grace had unexpectedly, given me the gift of the money.

"My goodness, what a lot of misery," Aunt May said. "Sounds like the money was a peace offering."

"I don't need to be paid to make peace."

"Hmmm, I think I see some of the problem. You always this prickly?"

"Well, Patty says I'm kind of like a cockle burr," I admitted.

"Sounds like she has the right of it. Well, the whole situation can't be easy on Grace, having to deal with that and all you kids all the time. No, no, listen now, I'm not taking her part. I'm just saying you have your part in it. Likely your Daddy has had all he can stand of being caught in between you two and he's backed off. I know my brother. He's a good man, but he's got his limits."

"Guess he does," I said miserably. "I guess he reached them with me."

"Maybe so."

We sat in silence, listening to the distant hum of traffic. Aunt May got up after a while and refilled our tea glasses. She sat back down heavily. We sipped it in silence. Finally, she said, "Well, guess it's up to you to fix it."

"I don't know how. He won't even listen when I tell him how sorry I am."

"Hmm. How are things between you and Grace?"

"We get along. Nothing to brag about. He's the same way with her right now."

"I'm right sorry to hear that. Not a good thing, with her being in the family way and all." She shifted in her chair. "That has got to be a heartache."

Her words made me feel guilty and even

worse than I already did about the situation. I sighed.

"I guess I'm the one who caused it all."

"No, I'd say that all of you have had your parts to play. You've been all wrapped up in your own pain, and your Daddy has run from his, and Grace just stepped right into a situation that no matter what good intentions she has, she can't fix. I don't know if any of you by yourselves can fix it. I do know this, though. She has been the soul of patience towards you, and if she lost her temper, then good for her. She needed to. I would have ripped into you long ago. That being said, I wouldn't step into her shoes for all the tea in China. Let's talk about something happier now, Tell me about the zoo trip and Spring Lake."

Knowing that the subject of my unhappy home life was closed as far as Aunt May was concerned, I complied. She laughed and laughed when I told her about the monkeys and about nearly losing our lunch on the roller coaster. I bet her she wouldn't ever ride it, and she laughed and bet me that she probably wouldn't ever ride it either. She took me in and showed me the project she was working on, a quilt for the new baby. Aunt May had never had any children of her own, to her sorrow. I always thought that was a shame, because I thought Aunt May was as close to perfection as someone could get.

When Patty and her mom came back for me at five, Aunt May hugged me hard and told me she would see me soon. I was surprised.

"You coming for a visit?"

"Yep. Think I'm going to come stay awhile and help out. John says I can go for however long I'm needed. Baby's due about the first of July, right?

"I think so."

"I'll come about the middle of June and stay until the baby's born. I imagine her Mama will come afterwards to stay and help her."

"I'm going to help too!" Patty enthused. "I love babies."

"I'll let you wash diapers," I teased.

"Nope, you'll wash them. I'm going to hold the baby."

"Well whatever you do to help, that will be wonderful," Aunt May smiled. "See you then. You have a safe trip home."

I couldn't wait. If anyone could make things better, Aunt May could.

CHAPTER TWENTY-SIX

School was almost over. It was that time of year when kids were tired of going to school and teachers were tired of kids that were tired of going to school. It was warm in the classrooms too. Sometimes the teachers, wilting in the afternoon's late spring heat, would let us go outside and do our work under the trees, where we had a chance to catch a breeze. As the days progressed, there was a sense of things ended and a promise of freedom. We couldn't wait. Patty and I laid plans for a swimming outing if she could talk her parents into driving to the big pool at Clinton. I was willing to lay bets she would be able to do so. Luke was headed to visit his mom in Tulsa for a visit after school was out. As usual, he didn't elaborate, and by this time we knew better than to ask him.

There was to be an all-school track day soon. Johnny and Georgie had been dashing up and down the drive to get ready and seeing how far they could jump. Lanie and Janie joined in until Lanie hurt her foot. After that she decided that she would just sit out and watch. I told her she would be healed by the time the track meet rolled around but she just looked at me sidewise and put on her pout face. For once, Janie decided to do something independently of her twin. For a little girl, she was really fast.

As for me, I had no intention of competing in anything. I wasn't fast, and I had always been the last girl picked for any team in the relay races. Sitting out was fine with me. Patty shared my dislike of physical exercise and planned on joining me in the bleachers. Luke was running in the relay races and participating in the broad jump. It was the first time I had seen him do anything athletic, since he hadn't participated in the basketball or football teams, and he had shown no interest in doing anything other than watching baseball. To my and Patty's surprise, he was swift and fleet-footed, leaving the other runners far behind at practice.

"Hey, you're pretty good!" Patty drawled when he plopped down on the bleachers beside us. "Who would have thought?"

"Well, not you, that's for sure," he said with a snort, and grinned to show he was just kidding. She stuck out her tongue at him. They had settled into a mutual love-hate relationship in which each insulted the other regularly. Sometimes I thought I needed to duck.

"Hey! Watch it!" Patty screamed as a water balloon went sailing over her head and landed with a wet plop next to her. I didn't know who had thrown it, but I was sure that we'd all be in trouble if we were caught. Luke shouted with laughter, that was cut off as a second balloon smacked him square in the chest. Patty and I giggled and he shot us a pained look as he took off after the one who had hit him in order to exact revenge with a water balloon that a near-by participant had handed him. By this time Coach Gage had become aware and was bellowing through the megaphone.

"Boys and Girls! Stop throwing those balloons! Right now!" He was promptly splattered with a balloon. We could hear him spluttering with indignation. Patty and I, after glancing at each other in consternation, quietly slipped off the bleachers and down the field. I didn't need to get in trouble at school. I think that would have been the final straw for Daddy. He was already angry with me over Luke.

I had come home and found him waiting for me. He told me to sit down in the kitchen chair and then stood there with his arms folded.

"What is this I hear about you hanging around with a boy?"

"Huh, oh, that's Luke. He's just a boy that hangs out with me and Patty."

"Just hangs out, huh? The person that told me that said it was more." He folded his arms and lowered his brows.

"Who told you that?" I was stunned. "We are just friends. He likes to talk to Patty and me, that's all."

"Annie Gibson, don't you lie to me!"

"I'm not!"

"Yes, you are."

"Whoever told you that is a liar!"

"Well, the person seemed pretty sure that

what they told me was the truth."

"And I'm a liar?" I stared at him, hurt. "I'm the one telling the truth, and you believe that person over me?"

Grace had come into the room, hearing our raised voices. She moved to Daddy's side and asked him to calm down. He ignored her.

"It occurs to me that you have something to hide," he said.

"It occurs to me that I have nothing, *nothing* to hide. I'm not even allowed to *talk* to a boy now?"

"Don't you talk to me in that tone," Daddy warned.

"Well you're telling me I'm a liar and I'm not," I said hotly. "Luke is just a friend."

"Luke, huh?"

"That's his name. He's Patty's friend too. You can ask her."

"Well you better stay away from him."

"That's hard to do. He sits by me in class."

"And at ballgames too, I hear."

"I won't deny that. He sits by Patty too, but whoever told you about him didn't bother to tell you that. Who told you anyway?"

"I was driving by and saw you on the bleachers with him. I didn't need to be told."

"So you just assumed the worst." I stared at Daddy in misery. It wasn't enough that he was acting coldly towards me. Now he had to make assumptions. "I told Luke a long time ago that I couldn't have a boyfriend. He accepted that. We are all just friends."

Daddy continued to eye me suspiciously. "Well that's all it better be. I think I'd better meet this boy."

"Well you can. We've got nothing to hide."

Grace chose this moment to speak. "We could ask him over to supper."

Oh lovely, I thought, *feed him and then rake him over the coals.* "I can ask him to come," I said.

"Who's his father? Do I know him? I may just want to have a word or two with him."

I could just imagine Daddy going to Luke's dad and telling him to have his son stay away from his daughter. My face flamed in anger.

"You'd be having words that don't need to be had. I'll ask Luke to come meet you."

Daddy folded his arms. "With all the trouble I've had out of you this past few months, I don't want to have to deal with you sneaking around with some boy behind my back. You hear me?"

"I haven't been sneaking!"

Trouble? I had gone out of my way to be good. I was dismayed at the total injustice of it.

"I haven't been any trouble to you or Grace for the past two months and all you want to do believe bad of me. I apologized for what I did and you are just being totally unfair to me now. You hate me!" I cried and fled up the stairs to my room and shut the door. I collapsed in a sobbing heap on the floor. It seemed no matter how much I did, I wasn't going to ever be in Daddy's good graces again. Grace's and Daddy's voices followed me up the stairs. Of all things, she was trying to reason with him. He wasn't having it. I heard him go out the back door, slamming it. Apparently what she said made him angrier.

He didn't come home in time for supper. Grace didn't say much of anything as we sat down at the table. Her mouth was compressed in a thin line of anger and frustration. She was careful not to say anything to me, nor did I say anything to her. It was just a bad situation all around. I struggled with the warring feelings of gratefulness that she had spoken up for me and with the resentment that she had mixed into the fuss between me and Daddy.

I helped her with the dishes and fled back up to my room to do homework while Lanie and Janie got ready for bed. For once, even they were subdued. Lanie was sucking her thumb, something she hadn't done in a while. I gently took it out of her mouth and gave her a kiss.

"Daddy was real mad, wasn't he," she asked, wide-eyed. Janie nodded her agreement.

"It will be okay," I told them.

"He's always mad at you. I wish he wouldn't be mad at you," Lanie said. *I wish he wouldn't always be mad at me too*, I thought.

They wrapped their arms around me and we sat on the side of the bed, holding one another.

It was about midnight before Daddy came home. I was awake. I imagine Grace was too. I could hear the rumble of his voice, no longer angry, down the hall, and her soft tones in answer.

The next day, I went determinedly to school and talked to Luke.

"Daddy thinks we're an item. You need to talk to him."

"Well aren't we?" he said jokingly, and then, noting my expression, his own became serious. "You mean he's mad?"

"Yes, he is. We had a big fight last night."

"Aw gee, Annie, I'm sorry," he said in consternation.

"You've got to go talk to him. He's wanting to go have words with your dad."

"Great. Just great."

"I told you how my Daddy was."

"Yeah, you did. I didn't think he'd have a fit over us just being friends."

"Well, Daddy and I aren't getting along too well anymore and he *wants* to believe I'm lying. Even Grace thinks he's being unreasonable, even though she doesn't like me," I mumbled, taking the books out of my locker and slamming the door.

"Well, what makes you think he'll believe me?" Luke said quietly.

"I thought that maybe if you and Patty told him that we were all just friends, he might," I said miserably. Luke just shook his head and walked off.

Patty was indignant when I told her. "What on earth is your Daddy thinking? We just hang out together, that's all."

"The worst he can."

"He's still mad at you, huh?"

"Yeah. He's always mad at me anymore. He doesn't ever hug me or talk to me or anything." The tears began to flow. "I don't have a daddy anymore *or* a mama. I feel so alone."

Patty wrapped me in a tight hug. "I'm so sorry. Look, I'll go over and talk to your Daddy and Grace. I don't know if Luke will, because he's such an odd bird, but I will."

She went to my house the very next day and talked to Grace about the situation. I waited in the next room while she talked to her. I heard Grace sigh and promise to talk to Daddy. Not that that would help much. He wasn't listening to her very much these days, either, she said. Patty promised to talk to Daddy if Grace needed her to. I wasn't sure that would help either.

Luke remained noncommittal about talking to Daddy. He didn't say he would, but he didn't say he wouldn't either. When I finally confronted him about it, he told me that he couldn't say we were just friends, because on his side, we weren't. I regarded him in shock. I had assumed we were just friends. Now what was I going to do?

He finally agreed to come and meet Daddy. I was on tenterhooks. Grace extended the invitation to dinner. I insisted that Patty come too. There was no need of making things any more awkward than they were already, I thought. Maybe Patty's presence would soften things a bit. Perhaps Daddy wouldn't unleash his temper on Luke if Patty were there. While Luke agreed to come to meet Daddy, there was one point on which Luke would not soften though.

"I'm not going to lie about how I feel about you. He'd spot that in a minute, and I want him to accept me when I do go to him. I don't want to start out with a lie,"

"Then you'd make me out to be a liar because I told him we were only friends!"

"Well, we are 'only friends.' That's what we are because that's where you keep it. I can tell him that, but if he asks anything else, I'll tell him."

I guess Patty and Grace did manage to convince Daddy that nothing was going on, so Luke was spared Daddy's temper when they finally did meet. Luke and Patty showed up on the appointed night to meet Daddy. To my surprise, Daddy was cordial, although not overly friendly. He shook Luke's hand, and Luke shook his back, looking him in the eye, which seemed to go over well. It was all very polite, although my insides were tied up in knots and I picked at my food. Patty and Luke seemed to have no trouble eating. Luke seemed to be at ease with the little ones. He was quite simply, himself, as always, under Daddy's scrutiny.

After dinner, Daddy took him outside on the porch to talk to him. I don't know what was said, but at least there weren't fireworks. When Luke left, Daddy issued an invitation for him to visit again. I nearly fell over with relief. At least he hadn't forbidden him to see me.

"I guess you can be friends," Daddy allowed grudgingly. "I told him there is to be no boyfriends until you are sixteen. He told me you'd told him."

See, Daddy, I didn't lie. I thought resentfully. *Why couldn't you believe me?* It was as though everything was poisoned by the fight with Grace. It felt as though he never wanted to believe in me anymore—that it was easier to believe bad of me than good. I stifled the hurt and said nothing in return. What was there to say?

Patty, behind his back, gave me a wink and a thumbs up. I knew she would have plenty to say when we were out of earshot of the grownups.

"See, I told you it wouldn't be so bad," she crowed. We had wandered down by the creek where we wouldn't be heard.

"There's no telling what Daddy said to him," I said miserably. "He'll probably not ever speak to me again."

"Oh, I'll bet he will. Really, Annie, you are so dense. Anyone with one eye can see he is crazy about you. Crazy enough to brave your daddy anyway," she laughed.

I glared at her. I felt really weird now, being around Luke, knowing how he felt. Our comfortable friendship wasn't so comfortable anymore and I was once more, tongue-tied in his presence. At least Daddy hadn't eaten him alive. That would have been one more mortification. I wasn't sure how I felt about him in return. I was relieved that school was almost over and that he was going away for a while, but a part of me was also sad too. Maybe he would forget me while he was gone. I didn't know if I wanted that.

Luke never did tell me what Daddy said to him, and I was afraid to ask. On the last day of school, he walked me to my locker and helped me with my things at the door. Then, defying all the rules and conventions that surrounded us, he bent and kissed me on the cheek and strode away, leaving me with my hand to my face, staring after him.

CHAPTER TWENTY-SEVEN

Summer weather set in with a vengeance around the first of June, humid and hot. If it weren't for the winds that blow all the time across the Oklahoma prairie, it would have been unendurable. I slipped down to the river as often as I could to splash and cool off and think about Luke. Sometimes Patty joined me, but she was helping her dad in their store and didn't get to come visit as much. Sometimes I managed to get free long enough to slip in for a Coca Cola and enjoy the sight of her officiating behind the counter. True to her word, we did get to go to Clinton to the pool, where we splashed and giggled with the latest music playing over the loudspeakers in the background. We stayed the night at Grandma and Grandpa Jenkins, who made much of us and took us out to dinner. Patty, in true Patty fashion, charmed them both. That was the highlight of the month. The rest of the days dragged on.

Daddy bought new excelsior for the swamp cooler and installed the cooler in the living room. Grace, heavily pregnant, spent most of her time on the couch there, trying to stay cool. She was increasingly miserable in the heat. I had had plenty of time to think of Aunt May's words, and I tried to ease the load of work she had. Daddy was still distant, saying little when he wasn't at work. He did bring home a television one night, to the delight of the whole family, and crawled up on the roof to install an antenna. That way, he said, Grace would have something to watch while she rested. She smiled and thanked him as the little ones settled down to watch a western on the small black and white screen.

I didn't have much time to watch the thing. I was too busy washing and ironing, and doing all the things that I had done the summer previously. I didn't see much of Patty at all now, because when she wasn't busy, I was. I heard that Luke had returned from Tulsa, although he didn't come around. Patty said he came into the store sometimes and ordered a Coke. She said he asked after me, but didn't say much about himself. I wondered if he had had a good time at his mother's. Once, in a rare burst of confidence, he had told me that his mother had "ran out on them." There was a world of anger in those words. He had sat silently, clenching and unclenching his fists. I hadn't known what to say to that or how to comfort him. After a while, he had looked up and shrugged off the mood and changed the subject. It wasn't mentioned again between us. With things the way they were right now, there really wasn't any way of knowing how the visit went. I knew he would not confide in Patty. I hoped that the visit had gone well.

Sometimes I thought despairingly that the endless round of chores I had to do was all I was ever going to spend my summers doing. Aunt May was now going to come the middle of July, but that seemed an eternity away. Grace did what she could, but it was increasingly hard for her to get around.

On the fourth, we set off fireworks in the driveway. We had had a makeshift picnic earlier in the day at my spot down by the river. Grace had begged off, but Daddy had come and brought the little ones to splash in the water and did some wading himself. He wasn't quite as cool and distant, but things had changed between us, and there was a gulf there now that neither one of us quite could get across. I watched him play with the boys, and wished I knew how to make things right again.

That evening, Grace dragged herself out on the porch and sat smiling wanly as the little ones squealed and twirled their sparklers and the boys set off Black Cats. It crossed my mind, that she wasn't having much fun either. I found myself feeling sorry for her, although my own self-pity was greater. Grace, as usual, seemed to sense what was going on in my mind and seemed troubled about it. Finally, a few days later, she said, "I want you to take some time this afternoon and just go have fun. Go see Patty. Go swimming. Just have fun."

"But I need to get things done around here. I don't want you to have to do them. What would Daddy say if he saw me? I have to keep on helping until Aunt May comes."

"I don't think they have to be done right this minute," she grimaced as she shifted position in the big chair that was now permanently stationed in front of the swamp cooler. "I don't think your daddy would object at all if you had a little bit of free time. You've been working really hard around here, and I feel really guilty that you have to do so much."

I thought of my quiet place down by the creek and the water, cool and inviting. "Are you sure?" I couldn't wait. All she had to say was, "yes" and I think I would have gone even if she weren't all right at this point.

"Yes, I'm sure."

"You won't do anything you shouldn't while I'm gone?" In spite of myself, I worried about her. This concern that was growing for her was unsettling. I told myself I would worry about anyone in her condition, but I worried, nonetheless.

"I promise I won't. You go and have a good time while the little boys and the twins are napping. Johnny and Georgie will be here. You can't pry them away from the television set, and your daddy will be home soon. I will be fine for an hour or two."

"All right, if you're sure."

"I'm sure," She shifted heavily in the chair again and made a face. "I'm just a little uncomfortable, that's all. I'll be glad when the baby makes an appearance!" She folded her legs under her and picked up the book she had been reading. "I may get this finished before then." She had been trying, without success, to get through *Gone With the Wind*. So far she was half-way through. Our eyes met, and we smiled. It had become a sort of joke that we could share safely without raising each other's hackles. She would fill me in on the story line while I did the dishes, or the laundry, or whatever she couldn't. I didn't know if she would make it through the book or not, but the way she re-told it was interesting.

I ran upstairs and threw on my creek clothes, pausing at the door to say thank you before I ran on out. Johnny caught me running across the yard, and immediately asked me where I was going. He wanted to go, and this time, I let him go without argument. He called out to Grace to let her know he wanted to go too. We asked Georgie if he wanted to go, but he didn't. For once he had the television to himself, and was settled down contentedly on the couch with a kitty on his stomach in the cool darkness of the living room.

We pelted down to the creek and jumped into the water, and splashed and yelled at each other wildly, then crawled out on the big rock to dry. I shook the water out of my hair and stretched full length in the sun, glad to have some time away from the endless chores I'd been doing. Johnny plopped down beside me and began picking red mud and grass from between his toes.

"Wish I could get out of the water and didn't have to do this," he grumbled.

"Well, if we went to a swimming pool, we wouldn't have to," I replied, "but this is free."

"Yeah, free grass and mud." He tilted his face towards the sun, squinting in the brightness of it.

"Frogs don't mind."

"Guess not. Guess I don't either." He got up and selected a rock and skipped it across the water. "You coming back in?"

"Does a catfish have fins? Come on."

We splashed around in the water a couple of hours before we headed back to the house. I knew I would pay for it in a sunburn and extra freckles, but it was worth it. The house was almost eerily quiet. There was no sign of Georgie and the girls. I wondered where they were. I went to the boys' bedroom to check on them and they were gone too.

"Grace? I'm back!" I called, knocking at the bedroom door. "Grace?"

"I'm here." Her voice was strained and soft.

I cracked the door to her bedroom open and saw that she was lying on the bed. The room was dim and cool. She was lying on her side with a cloth on her forehead.

"Where are the kids?"

"Your daddy took them to town for a while so I could get some rest."

"Oh. I should have stayed here, I guess."

"No. No. You needed to get out. Did you have fun?" She started to rise and sank back down on the bed, holding her stomach.

"I did. Are you all right?"

"I think so. I'm just really uncomfortable. It comes and goes."

"Where did Daddy take the kids?"

"I think he took them to Patty's house."

"Huh?" Why would he take them to Patty's? That was a strange outing, I thought. Suddenly, I realized what that might mean.

"The baby's coming?" I asked.

"I think so. Your daddy's going to take me to the hospital when he gets back."

"Why didn't he come get me and Johnny?"

"He felt you two were old enough to kind of watch yourselves," She shifted her position and grimaced,

"That wasn't what I was saying. He should have come got us so we could stay with you. What if the baby came?" Mama had had some of her babies really quickly. I was alarmed.

"I think it's going to take a while," Grace answered. "Anyway, I knew you would be back soon, so I sent him on. I will be fine," she added, seeing the look on my face.

"I'm glad you came in when you did, though. I was hoping you would get back in time to go with us, although I was afraid we'd have to leave you a note. Why don't you tell Johnny to get cleaned up, and you get cleaned up too so you can go?"

I was touched that she wanted us along. "I'll tell him," I turned and started out of the room. "I'll be right back."

In the grip of pain, she nodded acknowledgement.

Once out of the room I pelted outside and yelled for Johnny. He came out of the barn with a kitten in his hands. Georgie's kitty had blessed us with seven of them.

"What?"

"Grace is having the baby today.'

"She *is*?" His eyes grew wide.

"Put the kitty back in the barn and go get cleaned up. Daddy will be back any time now and we need to go. I get first dibs on the bathroom."

"You'll use all the hot water!" he complained.

"This time I won't. I promise. Now hurry!" He ran for the barn while I went back in the house. I took a shower in record time. Usually I would stand under the shower and just enjoy the feel of the water on my face and shoulders, but today I raced through and got dressed. He was waiting at the door and caught the clean towel and clean clothes I had gathered and thrown at him as I went out.

"Be sure to clean up your mess!" I told him.

"I will. I will!" *Sure he would. When pigs flew.* But there was no time to worry about that now. I'd take care of it after we got home.

"Good. Now get moving." I hurried into my bedroom and ran a brush through my hair and bundled it at the back of my neck. From the shower I heard Johnny singing "John Jacob Jingleheimer Schmidt" off key. I grimaced. Johnny certainly didn't win any awards in the singing department. I checked on Grace again. She reassured me that yes, she was fine. "Hurry!" I yelled up the stairs. A muffled, "I am!" came in response.

I heard our car turning down the driveway just as Johnny came out of the bathroom, his hair standing on end from the shower. Daddy came in the door and went into the bedroom. I fussed at Johnny to comb his hair, which he did with bad grace. It was enough, he mumbled, that he had to take a shower. I shushed him.

Daddy called to me from their bedroom.

"Annie, I want you to come and help Grace to the car. I've got to get the suitcase. Johnny, did you feed the dog and cats?"

"Uh, no, I forgot."

"You forgot. Well get out there and get it done. We don't have time to wait all day." Johnny raced off. Daddy shook his head and opened the closet door. "That boy."

"I'm going to be fine. There's no need to fuss," Grace said again as I helped her to her feet. She walked a few steps and clutched her stomach. Behind her back, Daddy and I exchanged a glance. We had been through this a few times with Mama and the last time had been a nightmare. Neither of us said a thing, but I'm sure he was thinking the same things I was.

Dogs and cats fed, Johnny joined us and hurled into the back seat beside me as Daddy settled Grace in. Daddy hopped in. The station wagon was slow to start. He swore and slapped the dashboard.

"Please, Thomas," Grace gritted out through another pain. He shot her a worried look before turning the start key again. This time the wagon shuddered into life and we shot out of the driveway.

"You know, I'd like to get there in one piece,

You'd think this was your first," Grace said dryly.

"He's always done that," Johnny said. I pinched him. "Ow! What did you do *that* for?"

"Shut up!" I hissed.

"Annie, just for once, especially now, can't you be nice?" Daddy shot me a look over his shoulder. I bristled. I *was* being nice. I was keeping Johnny from putting his foot in his mouth and reminding Daddy of the last time we took a trip to the hospital like this. I was remembering enough for both of us. It wasn't a good memory.

We had waited for hours the last time. Finally, the doctor had come out with a serious look on his face and told us that things weren't going well. That was an understatement. Mama had *died*. So had little Susanna. Remembering the pain of that day took my breath away. I clenched my jaw resolutely, willing the memory away.

Once we got to the hospital, which was thirty minutes away, they whisked Grace away behind a pair of folding doors, while Daddy completed the paperwork to check her in and then went back. Johnny and I sat in the pale green waiting room with the uncomfortable chairs that I remembered. I hadn't even thought to bring a magazine. I stared at the clock on the wall, utterly bored, while Johnny wiggled and squirmed and drove me half crazy. Finally, after I had counted all the ceiling tiles several times, Daddy came out.

"They're taking her upstairs, now. There's a waiting room up there. I've got to find a phone and call all our folks." He fished in his pocket for change and brought out a dime, and a couple of nickels. He sighed and pulled out his wallet. "I'm going to have to find some change for a dollar. Maybe the receptionist has some." He went to see. I turned to Johnny and saw that he had his sneakers off. Even worse, he had no socks on.

"Johnny, put your shoes back on!" I hissed. "You're embarrassing me."

"Okay, Okay."

Daddy came back with some change and we headed into the hall and got on the elevator. I hated that elevator. It always stopped with a lurch, and I felt like I was still rising or falling. I hung on to the rails. Daddy stared at the ceiling and whistled tunelessly under his breath. I didn't get my music skills from Daddy, I thought.

The elevator stopped with its usual shudder and we headed to the waiting room. Although Daddy was allowed to go in to see her for a few minutes, we had to stay there in the waiting room.

The wait seemed endless. Except for a brief foray to the hospital cafeteria to get something to eat, we stayed close. Daddy paced endlessly between visits. Johnny finally pushed two chairs together and went to sleep. I amused myself by counting everything in the room and trying to sing songs backwards. Every so often a nurse would come out and give us progress reports. So far, Grace was doing well.

I couldn't help going over and over the last time we came here: the hours of waiting, the doctor's grave face, his solemn tones, my world breaking into pieces with his words. I wondered if

Daddy was thinking about it. He was at the windows, staring out into the gathering twilight beyond, deep in his own personal world. I joined him at the window, and he slipped his arm around me. This was the first time he had shown me any kind of affection since we had had the fuss at Grace's parents' house. I leaned into the embrace and slipped both arms around his waist.

"I love you, Daddy,"

"I love you, too, Pumpkin." He patted my back. "It will be fine."

I knew then that he had been remembering. I moved out of his arms and looked out the window. In the west, the stars were beginning to come out. This time was so alike, and yet so different from the last time. It wasn't my mother in there this time. It was my stepmother. In spite of my differences with her, I wanted her to come through this. I didn't think I could face another funeral. I assured myself that she was young and strong in spite of her fragile appearance. Things would be okay. My new brother or sister would be here soon, I kept telling myself.

About nine, Nannie and Papa Smith came in. Johnny woke up and greeted them happily. After greeting Johnny and me with a peck on the cheek apiece, Nannie managed to get permission to go on back for a few minutes. Grandpa enveloped Johnny in a big, bear hug and slapped Daddy on the back. He tugged at one of my curls, which had come out of the loose ponytail I had bundled my hair into and smiled.

"How are you?"

"I'm fine," I smiled back. I liked Grandpa
Smith. I really did.

"Me too. I'm looking forward to holding my
baby's baby pretty soon." He settled himself in a
chair. "Tom, this gal gets prettier every time I see
her. You got your shotgun oiled?

"Shot gun?" Daddy sat down across from
him, stretched and yawned. "Why?

"To keep the fellows away," He looked at me
and winked. I blushed. My pained "Grandpa!"
made him chuckle. "She's growing up, Tom.
Won't be long until she's out the door."

"I'm in no hurry for that," Daddy growled.
Remembering the scene over Luke, I was sure he
wasn't. He had made that clear.

"I wasn't either," Grandpa winked.

Johnny came wandering up at that point and
Grandpa turned his attention to keeping him
occupied. From the depths of his overall pockets
he brought out a button and a length of string. The
wonders of what one could do with string and a
button kept them both busy for quite a while. I
slumped in a chair and stared at my fingernails.
They were ragged and bitten nearly into the quick.
I was going to have to stop doing that, I thought. If
my hands were any indication of how I looked, it
wasn't good.

Was I pretty? Not if my mirror was telling the
truth. I decided Grandpa needed glasses. I figured
Luke did too. Most of the boys I knew were
content with harassing me, but there was one who
acted as though he was interested. Mark Jones had
gone out of his way to talk to me, one day which

made Luke angry and caused Patty to laugh. I thought Luke was going to call him out, and Patty had teased me unmercifully. Patty and I nearly had our first fight over that one. I did *not have* a boyfriend, I told her. She just looked sideways at me and said, "Uh-huh."

That's not to say I hadn't ever wanted a boyfriend. I had had a mad crush on Tommy Reivers, for most of my eighth grade year. He never even looked my way though. I'd probably have been like a deer in the headlights of a car if he did, or dropped dead of sheer astonishment. He was a football player and moved in a much more rarified atmosphere than I did. Pretty girls surrounded him all the time: cheerleader and homecoming queen types. I wasn't either type. I was just plain old me. He was as far out of my orbit as Pluto was from the earth's.

I was brought out of my reverie by Nannie's entrance. She smiled at Grandpa, although her brow was crinkled with worry. She came over and sat down beside him and took his hand.

"Nurse chased me out, They're going to be taking her into the delivery room pretty soon. I declare, it's hard on a mama to watch her child go through that. No, Tom. You can't go in right now," She added when she saw Daddy stand up. "You may as well sit down."

Daddy sat.

"Is your mother coming up?" Grandma asked Daddy.

"I doubt it. It's a long way. She says she will come visit when everything settles down."

I wondered if she would even come then. Granny Gibson didn't come very often. It was hard for her to find a way to visit us, since she didn't' drive. Although she had managed to come for Thanksgiving, we hadn't seen her since then.

"I'm glad your sister May is coming down," Grandma said. "I could use the help."

"I called her. She will be on her way in the morning. She's said she will help out with the other children while you take care of Grace and the baby. Annie here could use a vacation. May was supposed to be here next week, but the baby has come a little earlier than we planned."

We settled down to a restless wait. Daddy paced back and forth, occasionally looking at his watch. I slumped in my seat and twiddled with a loose strand of hair, staring at nothing in particular. Grandma pulled a crochet project from her bag and kept her fingers busy. She offered to teach me how to do it, but I told her I didn't think I could settle down to concentrate. I finally pulled up a chair by the window, lay my head on my arms, and stared vacantly into space. Outside, the wind had picked up and clouds were scudding across a full moon. Johnny and Grandpa kept up a running commentary and told each other corny jokes. It was amazing how Johnny and he related to each other.

After a seemingly endless time, we heard a wailing cry from behind the closed doors down the hall.

"Can you hear the baby?" Grandpa said with a wondering look on his face. "The baby's here!"

He got to his feet. "Has a good strong set of lungs!"

We stared expectantly at the door and got to our feet when the doctor finally came out. He went to Daddy and shook his hand.

"Well Tom, you have a fine girl."

"And she's all right?"

The doctor, who had taken care of Mama on that last delivery, hastened to assure him. "More than all right. She's a big, strong, eight-pounder."

Daddy's face crumpled in relief. "How is Grace?"

"She's resting. She's been a trouper. We'll have the baby ready for you to see in a little bit."

"Thank God!" Daddy sat down and put his head in his hands. Grandpa Smith put his hand on Daddy's shoulder and patted it. Grandma Smith looked ready to march back through the doors and take care of her daughter herself, but stayed put and took up her crochet again.

"Another girl!" Johnny said in disgust. "I wanted another brother."

"Be quiet, you little twerp!" I hissed.

Daddy looked up and grimaced at Grace's parents. "Fred, what was that you said about her being grown up?"

"I didn't say she was growing up, only that she was growing prettier," Grandpa Smith chuckled. I stuck my tongue out at him and he made a funny face right back at me.

"A girl is just fine," I told Johnny, who scowled. I was so relieved that the delivery had gone smoothly. Somewhere at the back of my mind, in spite of my assurances to myself, I had been afraid that things weren't going to. I took a deep breath and let it out. I truly didn't care whether the baby was a boy or girl. I had plenty of both sexes as siblings. A baby was a baby, and this one was healthy. As long as I didn't have to go through another funeral, I could cope with another potentially bratty sister.

We were finally allowed to see her. They had turned the bassinet so we could see her through the nursery window and she was awake, swaddled in blankets looking placidly at her surroundings. She was red, and wrinkly, and had a shock of fuzzy red hair that proclaimed her a Gibson.

"Why look at that, Fred! She's got red hair like Annie's!" Grandma exclaimed.

"She does at that." Grandpa leaned in for a look.

"I can't wait to hold her," Grandma cooed. "Precious angel!"

Johnny, for a wonder, was awed.

"She's so little!" he said.

"Most babies are, "I said dryly. Surely he remembered how little Joey and Bobby had been.

"Oh shut up, Annie! You always have to be a smart-aleck," he said, but not meanly. He was too busy admiring our latest sibling to get really nasty.

"I thought you wanted a boy."

"She'll do. I'll teach her to climb trees and hunt frogs with me."

"Lovely. See, she's crying. She doesn't want to climb trees and hunt frogs with you."

"Yes she does," he insisted. "She's just crying

to get out of there and go."

The adults burst into laughter. I smiled in spite of myself.

"Welcome, little sister," I whispered to the baby, who had stopped crying and was regarding the world with big, solemn eyes. *The girls will go crazy over her,* I thought. I wondered what color her eyes would turn out to be. She had daddy's red hair, but she looked a lot like Grace. I gave myself up to the miracle of her coming, and for the moment, rejoiced that she was here, and whole, and well.

CHAPTER TWENTY-EIGHT

Grace and the baby came home from the hospital a few days later. Patty and her parents had stopped by and admired the baby at the hospital and then brought the boys home to stay with me, while Daddy stayed there at the hospital. Patty's mom had bought a fancy pink dress that was so frilled and beruffled that I was sure the baby would get lost in it. Patty was making big plans to camp at our house and love on the baby, which she had declared her honorary sister. I was waiting to see if the excitement would last when the baby threw up on her. Babies did that, I told her. She stuck her tongue out at me.

Aunt May arrived within a few hours of being notified and took over the household tasks with a vengeance. She and Nannie Smith set themselves to getting ready for the baby's homecoming. It didn't take me long to get tired from all the cleaning and running and fetching she and Nannie Smith had me doing. *You would think the Queen of England was coming home*, I thought resentfully. Every square inch of the house was scrubbed. Nannie Smith was determined that her first grandchild was going to come home to a house that was polished and cleaned and disinfected within an inch of its life. An array of sterilized bottles stood on the sink ready to be used, and there were piles of freshly washed diapers and rubber pants and nursery items all arranged neatly in regimented rows for handy retrieval. I didn't remember such a fuss when our other babies came home, I told Nannie Smith, and was rewarded with an indignant sniff. Aunt May's eyes twinkled at the exchange and she sent me on yet another errand, to my dismay.

Daddy, in the face of this relentless cleaning, learned to stay out of the way after being fussed at several times by his over-wrought mother-in-law. He took the boys and headed out to fish for a while before returning to the hospital. Lanie and Janie didn't escape. They were put to work folding diapers, and once they were done with the chore, they hid out in our room, from which indignant shrieks, as they settled whatever dispute of the minute, could be heard. I stayed out of there as much as possible. I hoped this new baby wouldn't grow up as bratty as those two. Grandpa Smith had gone home to take care of his animals, and, I suspected, to enjoy some peace and quiet before returning to greet his new granddaughter. I wished I could go with him. I would have even gone fishing, as much as I hated it, to get away. I was that desperate.

On the day Grace and the baby came home, we all gathered on the porch to wait for Daddy and Grace and the baby to arrive. The day was hot, but we were all anxious to greet the new member of the family. Aunt May had Janie and Lanie on either side of her, reading them a story. Bobby had found a roly-poly and was playing with it in rapt absorption. He was fascinated by them and would play with them for long stretches at a time. I had to physically restrain him from jumping into the dirt beside the porch to catch another when that one managed to unroll and escape. Heaven help him if he touched the baby with dirty fingers. Nannie would have gone nuts. Johnny and Georgie were trying out the slingshots Grandpa had gotten them. They had already had one stern warning from the adults about shooting the twins, who divided their attention between the story and watching the boys warily.

A little after mid-morning, the station wagon pulled into the drive. Johnny was the first to see them coming and gave out a whoop. Daddy hopped out and ran around and opened the door. Somehow Grandma Smith was there before anyone else, waiting to take the tiny, pink-blanketed bundle from him as he handed it out of the car. All of the little ones came boiling off the porch to see and gathered around Nannie Smith, hopping up and down, trying to get a peek at their new sister. Lanie and Janie were in raptures, thinking of this new sibling as a sort of fancy doll, although they had been warned that she was a person and not a plaything. I imagined the baby wouldn't lack for entertainment if they had their way. They were already arguing, as they had many times before, over who would get to hold her first, or who she would love best. Georgie hadn't said

much, but he let me know he was going to give
her one of his kitties. Those kitties meant the
world to Georgie. I had hugged him and told him
what a thoughtful thing he was doing.

"Get back, now!" Daddy warned as he helped
Grace out of the car. "You'll all get a chance to see
her. Let's get Grace in and her settled. You'd think
they'd never seen a baby before," he said to
Grandpa, who chuckled.

"Not this one anyway," Grandpa had taken the
baby from Nannie Smith and was cradling her as
though she were a precious piece of glass. "Going
to have to count her fingers and toes to make sure
she's a keeper."

"Fred Smith! What a thing to say! But I'll
help you count them." Grandma Smith scolded
and then laughed. She tenderly tucked back the
folds of the blanket and gazed into the face of her
granddaughter, face alight. They and Daddy and
Grace went on in the house, trailed by the children
and Aunt May. I stayed outside. I figured I would
hold her later, when the new wore off for everyone
else. I intended to enjoy a few minutes of peace.

It didn't last long.

"Annie?" Grace called from inside.

"Yes, ma'am?"

"Could you come in here a minute?"

"Guess so." I wondered what she could want.
I went into the living room. I found her seated in
the big chair. Grandpa had given her back the baby
and she had her cradled on her lap.

"I need you to come here. Sit down right here.
Can you hold your sister for me a minute?"

Could I hold her? Yes, I could.

I held out my arms and she placed the baby in them. I looked down into the little sleeping face with its frame of red fuzz and felt something tight in me unwind. I touched the petal soft cheek in wonder.

"I guess you want to know what we named her."

"What?" Daddy and Grace hadn't told any of us what she was named. They wanted it to be a surprise, they said.

"How do you feel about the name Melissa Ann Marie?"

Ann—that was Mama's name, and mine. I looked up in amazement.

"Why are you asking me?"

She was smiling at me.

"Because she will have your name, I wanted to know how you felt about it."

"Why chose my name? Shouldn't she have one of her own?"

"It will be her own."

"Why?"

"I wanted to thank you for all the things you've done for me. I know we haven't had an easy relationship, and at times it's been downright hostile, so I wanted to do something to show how much I love you for what you do," Grace's eyes met mine across the baby's head. Her expression was warm and loving. "You are a fighter, Annie. You've overcome so much. I want your sister to have some of that spirit, so I gave her your name to always remind her of that sister."

I felt my breath catch in my throat. Through
tears that suddenly welled up and gathered,
threatening to spill over, I said, "That's fine. Just
don't call her Annie too. She should be called her
own name." I kissed the baby and busily arranged
the folds of her blanket. "I don't know what to
say."

To think that this woman, whom I had
resented and fought tooth and nail, wanted to
name her baby after me. I was quite overtaken by
the wonder of it all.

"Well, why can't she be named John Marie or
something? Gee," Johnny broke the moment.
"And when am I going to get to hold her?" The
grownups laughed. I smiled through the lump in
my throat.

"Right now, if you promise not to take her
frog hunting," Grace laughed. He sidled over and
held out his arms. I put the baby into them. He
held her stiffly at first and then suddenly cuddled
her to him. I would never have thought I'd see the
day—Johnny going soft over a baby, but there he
was holding his face close to hers and whispering
to her as though she could understand him. I was
sure he was telling her about all the fishing and
frog hunting he was going to teach her to do. I
hoped she wouldn't disappoint him.

All the little ones got to hold and love on the
baby before Grandma Smith and Aunt May
whisked them away to the bedroom to rest before
we had our noon meal. At loose ends, I wandered
outside and plopped down in a chair. Johnny
followed me and lay on his stomach, trailing his

arm from the porch to trace patterns in the dirt.

I truly didn't know what to think. They had named the baby after me? Grace was full of surprises. I was definitely surprised. It was good of her, I guessed.

"You know what?" Johnny's question broke into my thoughts. "Melissa Ann is going to be the best frog-hunting girl in the country."

I laughed. If he had his way, she surely would.

"Don't laugh. You'll see."

"Why are you so set on teaching her to frog hunt. She's a girl. You have brothers already. You can teach them to frog hunt."

"Don't know. I just think I want to."

"Why don't you take Janie and Lanie frog hunting?"

"Those two!" the words held a world of scorn. "They'd scream and cry and say 'ewww.'"

"They probably would."

"Annie?"

"What."

"Do you care that they named her after you?"

"It will take some getting used to."

"I think it's sort of nice." With a swing of wild arms, he was off the porch. "Come on, Annie. Let's go to the creek!" He strolled down the driveway, stopping to look over his shoulder. "Come on, Annie!"

"It's almost time to eat."

"I know, but we can go for a little while."

"You go on. I'll be there in a bit."

He shrugged and pelted down the drive on his way to the creek, his heels stirring up eddies of red dust as he ran. I laid my head back against the chair and closed my eyes, thinking of Mama, thinking of all of us, and the new baby.

Aunt May had been right. Grief was kind of like a journey to a far country—one that you took a while to come back from. I had been on that far journey, but somehow, the arrival of this newest sister had helped me find some solace. Perhaps, I could turn around and begin the journey back. In naming the baby after me, Grace had reached out in peace.

The time she had spent in labor and my fears for her had taught me that I didn't really hate her. Perhaps it was okay to love her just a little bit without being disloyal to Mama? Perhaps I could make some room in my heart for this woman who had stepped into my life and tried to be my friend. She didn't have to take my Mama's place, but she could stand beside her in my heart, I imagined Mama smiling at that and approving.

I opened my eyes, hoisted myself up from the chair and hurled myself off the porch. Johnny had stopped and was waiting for me impatiently.

Smiling, I ran to join him.

Meet Our Author
Ruth Ramsey

Ruth Ramsey was born and raised in western Oklahoma and grew up travelling on Route 66. She has spent the majority of her life in various towns in Washita and Custer County except for a brief time living in Wyoming. She received a Bachelor of Arts in English Education in 1988 from Southwestern Oklahoma State University, graduating *summa cum laude*, and has since pursued a teaching career. She currently is completing her twenty-second year of teaching in a rural school in southwest Oklahoma, where she teaches English and Art and is the yearbook advisor. She also has a background in journalism, having served as a women's editor for the Clinton Daily News, Clinton, OK, a columnist and stringer for the *Woodward News*, Woodward, Oklahoma, and as a features writer and contributing editor for the *Casper Star Tribune* and the *Casper Journal*, Casper, Wyoming, respectively. She also writes poetry, and has had her work published in *Westview Magazine.* She is an avid amateur genealogist, draws portraits of people, whose faces she finds endlessly fascinating, and has been active in community theatre as an actress and director, as well as singing in local community choirs. *A Far Journey* is her first novel.

Made in the USA
Coppell, TX
25 August 2020